His fiction, poetry and translations have appeared in various international journals including *Granta*, *Vallum*, *The Caravan* and *Words Without Borders*. He was selected as a *Granta* new voice in 2011 and was named an Honorary Fellow of the International Writing Progarm at the University of Iowa. *The Scatter Here is Too Great* was awarded the Shakti Bhatt First Book Prize and was shortlisted for the DSC Prize for South Asian Literature. Bilal Tanweer lives in Lahore.

BILAL TANWEER

The Scatter Here is Too Great

VINTAGE

2 4 6 8 10 9 7 5 3 1

Vintage
20 Vauxhall Bridge Road,
London SW1V 2SA

Vintage is part of the Penguin Random House group of companies
whose addresses can be found at global.penguinrandomhouse.com.

Penguin
Random House
UK

Copyright © Bilal Tanweer 2014

Bilal Tanweer has asserted his right under the Copyright, Designs and
Patents Act 1988 to be identified as the author of this work

First published in India in 2013 by

Random House Publishers India Private Limited

First published in Vintage in 2015

First published in hardback by Jonathan Cape in 2014

www.vintage-books.co.uk

A CIP catalogue record for this book is
available from the British Library

ISBN 9780099589846

Printed and bound by Clays Ltd, St Ives plc

MIX
Paper from
responsible sources
FSC   FSC® C018179
www.fsc.org

Penguin Random House is committed to a sustainable future for
our business, our readers and our planet. This book is made
from Forest Stewardship Council® certified paper

For Amma, Zain and Amna,
for your prayers, love and support;
I owe you everything

Contents

We are continually living a solution to problems
that reflection cannot hope to solve.

—Van den Berg

Bashō told Rensetsu to avoid sensational materials.
If the horror of the world were the truth of the world,
he said, there would be no one to say it
and no one to say it to.
I think he recommended describing the slightly frenzied
swarming of insects near a waterfall.

—Robert Hass, 'Winged and Arid Dark'

THE SCATTER HERE IS TOO GREAT

Ever seen a bullet-smashed windscreen? The hole at the centre throws a sharp clean web around itself and becomes crowded with tiny crystals. That's the metaphor for my world, this city: broken, beautiful, and born of tremendous violence.

One way to give you this account is to 'name the streets and number the dead'. Another is to give you this scatter I have gathered: to make sense of things, go beyond appearances, read the crystal design on the broken screen.

My mind is a stiff skein of voices. I will yank out the threads and find the edges.

Listen.

A WRITER IN THE CITY

Blackboards

I HAVE PROTRUDING TEETH and because of this everyone at school called me parrot, parrot. One day I beat up this one boy who called me parrot, parrot even though I did not say anything to him. He had short brown hair. I caught him by his hair and then I beat him. But I did not know I said bad words to him and his father and his sister too. This happens when I am angry. One of the other boys later told me I used the sister-word to abuse that boy with brown hair, his father and his sister. He said that I said bhenchod to him. It is not a word I would say. Not to his father. But everyone says that I said this word. Everyone cannot lie.

My teacher called Baba to school. Baba did not believe that I knew the words my teacher said I used when abusing her and the boy. She said I abused her when she was trying to pull me away from the boy. I had pulled him down with his hair and climbed on his chest and slapped his face many times. In return, he scratched my face with his nails. I remember all this but not the swearing.

At first, Baba doubted the teacher, but when other people also told him that they heard me abusing, he was angry and stopped talking to me. I said sorry, sorry to him so many times but he would not say anything or even look at me. Then I became angry and started to cry. And I shouted at him as well. My sister and mother were very scared when I was shouting at Baba. My mother was eating when I was shouting; she stopped chewing her food and just kept looking at me. I saw her looking but I only knew I was angry and I was crying. I did not know what I was saying. Amma beat me with the big steel spoon for getting angry at Baba. Also because I shouted at him. She had bought this spoon from the bazaar two days back and it was dipped in the curry bowl. When Amma hit me, it was hot and I could smell the curry on my hand all night. But I was already crying so her beating did not do anything to me. There were red marks on my arms later. But I am strong. After that everyone became quiet. I was sitting alone on the sofa. My mother took my sister in a corner and told her to make me eat food because I had not eaten. They thought I did not know what they talked about in the corner. But I knew. My sister came with the food. She fed me food with her hands, and she told me that I should say sorry to Baba.

I apologized but nothing really happened. He kept quiet. He said to Amma, 'I do not know where he learnt this language. He is so small.'

Baba had two jobs. He worked in office and he wrote

little books of stories. He said he wrote them for kids like me. I told him I was not a little kid. He read me all his stories. They were in little eight-anna books and they were all about brave people who fought bad people.

Very few people at school fight. But that is because no one calls them parrot, parrot. Soon I left that school. Not only because of fights but because Amma said it had a bad environment. Then Baba started to teach me. He taught me everything in stories. He showed me how all numbers were animals and you have to watch them do things and say what has happened to them at the end of the story: Plus means animals gather together. Minus means they leave each other. Multiply and divide happen when there are different types of animals. It's easy: 4 x 2 means there are 4, 4 animals of 2 kinds, like 4 sheep and 4 cows, and together they are 8. And divide happens when you have to find out how many groups are there of each one of them.

At school I had problems learning spellings and tables. Baba taught me about the blackboard we have in our minds, and we can use it to draw in our heads with coloured chalk. I used to close my eyes and draw on the blackboard. And whenever I wanted to remember spellings, I copied them from the blackboard. After that I did not find it difficult to remember things. I even drew things on the blackboard when I went to sleep at night.

I taught Baba to draw on the blackboard also. When he came back from the office, I took off his glasses, sat on his stomach, and then we closed our eyes. Initially,

Baba drew only sceneries: one house and one sun and six hills. But then I explained to him that we had a big board, and we could draw *anything*, with any colour. So then we drew Pakistan's flag. I drew small flags, I liked them. Baba said his flags were large. While drawing, I would sometimes forget what I was drawing and listen to the chalk's sounds—*tak-takka-tak-tak* and sss-*hisssss*. But I did not tell Baba this. I knew he would not understand. I just told him to make things: fish, grass, stars (they were the easiest), a big-sized sun. I would always make three suns: one sun for the morning, one for the evening, and one for the night. Whatever scenery I made, I had a sun there. I liked the sun. Sun contains light in it. I liked bulbs as well. Bulbs are suns. Small suns. But I like the big sun that no one can turn off. Sometimes, I would just tell Baba to fill his blackboard with light. We did this with yellow chalk. Then one day, just like that, Baba and I started drawing cars and big houses, with big terraces. We chose different colours for rooms and cars. And then, when we finished drawing, we would tell each other what our cars looked like, what the shape of the windows was, what all we could see outside, what colour the floors in the house were. I always told Baba about my drawing first because if he told me his I would forget mine.

After I finished my homework, Baba told me stories from storybooks he brought from his office. My favourite story was a story Baba wrote himself. It was about a brave little blue fish who was a boy like me and who lived in a pond and goes to the big river and meets other big fish and helps them. It is a story about being brave and always saying the truth. After reading the stories, Baba smoked his special tobacco, which made hot white smoke, and then with the smoke and his fingers made animals in the stories—little ducks, sparrows, eels, snakes, other fish. It sometimes made him cough a lot and Amma said it was bad for him and I should not make Baba do things that were bad for him.

I also left school because we had become poor. Baba lost his job at the office where they printed children's storybooks. Baba wrote some of those storybooks, like the story of the blue fish. And the new job was not good. The old uncle Baba worked for was shot while walking out of a bank. Two people on a motorcycle tried to snatch his money. When he refused, they shot him. After that, uncle's brother took over the business. But he did not like Baba because Baba always spoke the truth.

That night I heard Baba saying to Amma, 'I don't think they are happy with me. I had a fight today as well. No, they did not say anything. I just don't like to fight the family I have worked for all my life. His brother and his family have been our guardians for the past eight years. But if they want to change their ways, I don't know how I will get along.' Amma was quiet. Everyone was sleeping. They were talking in the dark in low voices. My sister was sleeping, but I was awake. Baba and Amma talked every night like this. Baba said little and then Amma said little.

And then they would turn quiet. And then they would say little, little things again and again. And then everyone would go to sleep.

On the day I shouted at Baba, he was completely quiet that night. Amma said, 'He is so small. He will learn.' Then she went silent for some time. I thought they were asleep. She spoke again, 'Someone must have taught him at school.' I heard her hand rubbing Baba's chest. 'You must not worry so much about him. He is so small.' Usually they laughed lightly when they talked about me. But that day Baba was not saying anything to Amma. Just like he was not saying anything to me. I heard him breathe. He said, 'I think we will have to take him out of school. I don't think I will have this job for too long.'

I felt Baba was drawing a night on his blackboard; a night with a lot of rain and the wet lights of cars, but no sun.

Before we were poor, we used to go out to some nice place to eat every week. I liked that place along the sea where I had spicy barbeque chicken. My chicken piece was so spicy that I used to get tears. But then we became poor. But Amma tells me I should not say we are poor. After all, we have enough to eat and drink, and have a place to sleep and we are better than millions. So one day when I started crying, Baba told me, 'Don't cry, don't cry. Let us go to the sea on the bus.' I had not been on the bus before, so

I was happy and wanted to go with Baba. Baba says that it is one and the same sea everywhere around the world, but he also says there are only very few cities that have the sea. Karachi has a sea.

Amma made me wear my nice dress-pants and put a lot of powder on me so that I would not get skin rash from the heat.

The bus did not stop. It moved and we had to sit in it while it was moving. Baba lifted me onto the bus, the conductor pulled me in, and then running, Baba also got onto the bus. The conductor was the last one to get in. It was dangerous. My heartbeat grew fast. At such times I do not feel good. Our doctor-uncle has told me not to play too hard, and not to fight. Because then I become ill for long. And because old uncle is not here, Baba will have to pay the doctor's fee. Old uncle always used to pay our doctor's bill.

Baba paid the conductor, who had all the money in his hands. I asked Baba, 'Why doesn't the conductor keep the money in his pockets?' Baba said because there is too much of it and someone might steal it from his pocket. But why don't people steal from his hands? Baba said because he is always watching his hands. When you don't want your things to be stolen, you must always watch them. We were sitting at the back of the bus, and Baba was looking out of the window. The bus seats were red and looked dirty. I did not touch them but I was sitting on them. There were designs on the roof with glitter on them. I closed my eyes, opened my blackboard and made those same designs in one of the rooms in my house. The big eagle, white horse with wings, lots of green hills, a big light-pink rose in the middle of the green hills, and shining gold, red, ruby red colours surrounding them. It is difficult to make shiny things on blackboards, but I had a trick. I threw water on the chalk to make it shiny. The floor of the bus was dirty. It had grease-like things all over it. You should not draw dirty things on the blackboard.

The man sitting next to us leaned out of the open door, which is always open, and spat out every few minutes. I looked away. Baba did not even notice the man, who wiped his face with his sleeve after spitting.

The bus was going very fast and the wind blowing in from the windows was very hot. So I hid myself behind Baba. It was like being in a shadow. Shadows are empty places in things. The colour of shadows is also black, which is the colour of empty things. Blackboard is also black when it is empty. No one can draw shadows on blackboards because shadows keep on changing. You cannot draw changing things. But this happens, you know; you draw and you look and it has changed.

Then a fat man without a leg got on the bus. He was even fatter than Baba. He was smiling. He got on the bus and made a joke, 'Aray bhayya! Slow down! If I fall out of the bus, my wife will not wash my clothes!' Everyone smiled. The conductor also smiled. He paid the conductor in coins. The conductor gave him a discount.

The fat man without a leg looked at me and smiled and gave me a cow-toffee. It made me think of my Comrade-uncle who also brought cow-toffees for me when he came to see Baba. Baba told Amma that he was a sad man. 'He left his family and everything for his work. He keeps thinking of them but I don't think he realizes that.' I knew he was sad because he smelled sad like tired and sweat mixed.

The fat man without a leg was a nice man. My Comrade-uncle is also nice. He was even nicer when he lived with his family. He was tall and everyone liked him. He brought me toffees; many kinds of toffees, and biscuits. The skin under his eye is black because he fought the police. He does not say his prayers. He says there is no Allah. Many people say he is so sad and without his family because of that. He shouts at them who tell him to pray. He was not like this before. He used to smile. He is a communist. That's the name of people who do not pray.

The fat man asked me my name, my school and what I would become when I grew up. I told him I will be a pilot and fly fighter planes and fight with India. He told me that fighting is not good, and told me to fly planes to carry people from one place to another. I said but those planes do not fly fast. He said they are very fast. I said but I do not like the way they looked, like eggs. I told him I did not like egg-planes. He started laughing. His stomach moved even more than Baba's when he laughed. His teeth were very dirty. He gave me the cow-toffee. Baba said I should thank him. Then Baba told the fat man about me. He said this boy is very naughty and loves to fight and beats his classmates. I said that is because they call me parrot, parrot.

Then I went to sleep. Baba put his arm around me and I was in the shadow and the hot wind coming in through the door did not touch my face and I went to sleep. I woke up when someone was shouting. Three thieves had come in the bus. One of them sat next to the back door, on Baba's side. The other was at the front door. And the third one stood in the middle with his gun. They all had shiny guns and their faces were covered with cloth, which kept falling away. (We all saw their faces. One of them had a thin moustache. The other had a thick, short beard; he was chewing the hair of his lower lip.) The one standing in the middle of the bus was shouting loudly. We were all scared. He said, 'Close the windows!' One window would not close. It was stuck. The thief was shouting at the man sitting next to that window asking him to shut it. I was so scared. I thought the beard-thief would shoot this man for not shutting the window. But then he told him to leave it. He also told the conductor to close the doors.

The bearded thief shouted at us, 'Whatever, whatever you have, drop it on the floor in front of you. If I find anything near anyone, I swear to God, I will fire a bullet through his head without a thought.' The thief sitting next to us stood up and started taking everyone's money. He

14

took it first from Baba. I wanted to fight him. But I was scared. No one stood up to fight him.

The thief who was at the front sitting with the driver said to the ladies in the front compartment, 'Do not fear. You are like our mothers and sisters. We will not bother you. We do not need your money.' When he said this, the fat man said, 'Please let us go. Aren't we like your brothers and fathers?' The thief thought that the fat man was trying to make fun of him. He looked at him straight in his eyes, 'What did you say? *Haan*?' and then slapped him. It made a loud sound. He put the gun on his head, 'You find this very funny, *haan*? *Funny*, haan?' And he slapped him again. Everyone turned to see the man being slapped. It was like in the class. When the teacher slapped one boy, no one spoke again.

The thieves took all the money but kept riding the bus with us. They took the money from the conductor. The conductor was watching his notes when the thief took them from him. One of the thieves took the money and put it in his bag. Everyone was looking at them doing this.

Then one thief started telling the driver where to go and how to drive, when to slow down, when to drive fast. He also hit the driver once on his head; it did not make any sound. The slaps on the fat man's face were louder. The thieves took the bus very far and after driving for a long time they told the driver to stop. And then suddenly two thieves quickly jumped out and the third thief started shouting at the bus driver and everybody else. 'IF somebody steps out, we'll shoot straight in their head. NOBODY comes after us NOBODY. UNDERSTAND?' When he shouted like that I hid my face under Baba's arm.

The bus driver then drove so fast and everyone on the bus stayed quiet because we were all afraid that the thief who was shouting might shoot us from behind the bus.

The bus driver stopped the bus at the sea, and said it would not go any further. 'Get on other buses if you want to go anywhere.' Everyone suddenly became angry. They started to fight with him because thieves had taken their money.

Baba and I got off at the sea. The fat man without a leg was also going to the sea. He was not smiling now. His face was red. Baba had a secret pocket in his shalwar where he always hid some money. He gave a few notes to the fat man. Then he took me to the sea.

We sat on the shore and watched the waves that came so slowly. There were few people there and the wind was cool. I wanted to go on a camel ride, but I knew that Baba did not have the money for that. Baba was quiet. I felt he was drawing the night without a sun on his blackboard again. So I snuggled under his arm and said, 'Baba, let us draw even bigger camels than there are here.' I was so afraid to close my eyes because it was getting darker and I was afraid that new thieves might come. But I think it made Baba happy. When I drew the camels, Baba said, 'Let us sit on these camels as well!' So I sat on my very, very big camel. I rode on it. And when Baba asked me, 'How does it feel riding such a big camel?' I said, 'It is like riding on waves.'

Evening came. Baba and I sat on a bench and had roasted peanuts. Baba asked me if I was afraid of the thieves. I told him I was not. I wanted to fight them. He smiled. He told me never to fight thieves and if something like this ever happens 'just give them everything without saying anything.'

When we were returning home, we took the bus again. This time I ran and got on the bus myself without the conductor's help. On our way, we passed that place where we used to have barbeque and where my chicken was the spiciest. I put my head on Baba's arm and he put it around me and I was in the shadow again. As I closed my eyes, I imagined my blackboard as big as the sea on which I drew a ship—a big ship moving on waves like a camel. And then I saw the cloth with which the thief covered his face, which kept on slipping and revealing his face. I wanted to draw a sun in the sea because it was dark and I wanted to give light to the ship, but then I fell asleep. But I remember the ship looked like an empty place, like a shadow, and the cloth was fluttering in the wind like its flag.

SUKHANSAZ

After That, We Are Ignorant

YESTERDAY, AN OLD MAN, bloody idiot, surely off his rockers, got on the bus from the Lucky Star stop... tall in his height, some six-three, wore a new, bright red Coca-Cola cap that you get for free these days, bloody joker. His shirt, I think he had been re-ironing since the creation of Pakistan. His crumpled brown pants seemed straight out of the washing machine. He caught my eye as soon as he got on the bus. I pulled out my sketchbook and started to make his cartoon. The rectangular golden frame of his spectacles covered his long, thin face. Acha, at first he did not say anything, just took a seat, sat there and looked around. Then he turned to the guy next to him and without any, what's-its-name, any hesitation, questioned him, 'Who are you?'

At this, the guy was startled and he looked at him cluelessly. Obviously, bhenchod! Anyone would jump at such abruptness...If someone asked you who you are, randomly, just like that, on the bus, and that too, a weird-looking old creep wearing a red cap and shirt with broken buttons, what would *you* say?

But that guy was some bugger, he smiled and replied, 'I am a human, thank you,' and shook the old man's hand. Hehe. Bastard. Guess what the old man did? He just said, 'Okay,' and turned away. I was laughing to myself from my seat and seeing me, others also got interested in what was going on. I felt the old man was no less than a cartoon himself. He was staring at the back of the seat in front of him—like this—his face completely blank—like this. And then after staring for a few seconds he turned back to the guy he questioned earlier and said, 'I am Comrade Sukhansaz! Happy to meet you!' and pushed out his hand towards him.

Now whatever the hell is a comrade! Most people don't even know what these creatures are. There was a time when these Comrades and Reds and Lefties were a common breed you'd find on the streets, but that general, Zia, that dog of the CIA, he ate them all up. He liked blood, that dog. Where else do you think all this Islam and drugs and guns and bombs came into this city? They are a recent invention, my love. Americans gave him the money and guns and a carte blanche for drugs to fight the Soviets, and he fucked the country and this city for his jihad next door, thank you. Yes, you do find some Comrade occasionally, still bitten, his ass still bleeding and bandaged. All of them hate Zia. Haha! I mean whatever but you've got to admire Zia for the treatment he gave them—jail, torture, lashing them in public, haha! The joker even put his own name in the constitution! He used to see things in his dreams and made them his policies. Yup, Americans loved his dreams because he was screwing the Soviets and Comrades in them. So yeah, most Comrades are dead now.

So guess what that guy said when the Comrade said, 'I am Comrade Sukhansaz'? He was some smartass, he returned a dumb expression, and asked, 'Sukhansaz, that's the word for poet...But what's your *name*? And what's Comrade...Is that a Muslim name?'

Hahaha! What's-his-name, Comrade, he turned red, even though technically that wasn't possible because he was so dark, but oh, you should have seen his face—imagine a dry, savage brown flashing with colour! At first Comrade Sukhansaz didn't reply, just turned his face and stared at the back of the seat. After a few moments, he began blabbering in a low voice. 'In this country, everything is either Muslim or non-Muslim, everything, everything. Is your shoe Muslim? This cap, does it go to the mosque with you? Does your spoon and knife say their prayers on time? Everything, bloody everything is Muslim or non-Muslim! Is this colour a Muslim colour? And then no one can talk about religion...names, now names are Muslim and non-Muslim!'

That I-am-human fellow was acting like a smartass but really you should have seen his face, nervous like hell. I mean what do you expect when you are sitting next to this nut case? The Comrade turned to him again and said, 'I am a poet. I was in jail. Yes, jail. For eight years. People love me. You know they love me. They know me. The whole world knows me.' He fell silent and looked around the bus. He saw us sniggering, all thoroughly entertained.

Praise be the worm up my ass, I shouted, 'Haan, so mister Comrade Sukhansaz, let us hear something, some poetry, some of your amazing verses...' And oh brother, I tell you, the moment I finished my sentence, he sprang into action, as if he had been waiting. He stood up, and then holding his seat with one hand, like this, his fingers all twisted backward, started reciting poems, one after another...I cannot tell you. And he was so good! I remember a few lines:

> *The argument between this lover with the other*
> *is who loves more. After this, both are ignorant.*

> *The tussle of this believer with the other*
> *is how to worship. After this, both are ignorant.*

> *The brawl of this politician with the other*
> *is how to gain power. After this, both are ignorant.*

It turned into a circus soon when a group of college students sitting at the back of the bus started to make noises in between his recitation. Each time Comrade Sukhansaz paused between the couplets, they made a sound: *Dha Dha Dha Dhayyn...* like those Hollywood action movie soundtracks. At first Comrade was confused, because some of us were actually enjoying the poems and praising them as well, but soon the boys began to rattle him. He ignored it a few times, but then suddenly, haha! I remember he was saying: *We will win against darkness too!* And then he broke off yelling, 'Abay O rowdy idiots! Listen to what I am saying!'

It was so funny—abay! Listen to me! I am telling you about darkness and winning!

For the boys, well, this was what they were looking for to begin with. It added to their fun and then they started purring and barking in between his verses. You got to love their timing! Imagine a dog's whimper—*aaoo aaoo aaoo*—as if someone has kicked it in its gut—after *both are ignorant.*

Comrade got really riled though. He stopped abruptly and took his seat, muttering under his breath. And then the whole bus broke into applause, clapping for him. I whistled... You know the one I whistle, the long loud one. I shouted, 'One more Comrade, one more!' But he didn't pay attention and continued to blather to himself in a low voice and kept staring at the back of the seat. Haha! Old bugger. The man sitting next to me was looking over my drawing. He said to me, smiling, 'Why tease the old fellow. Let him be...' Well, I really didn't give a toss about him or his poetry... for me, I had to finish up my sketch. He was a God-sent cartoon on the bus. What more can a cartoonist ask for? I had to do him for my records.

I was trying to get his nose right but he turned his face the other way. I waited but then I got impatient. I shouted, 'Comrade, you old man, have you forgotten your poetry?' That really got him! He turned immediately and began shouting, 'Who said that? Haan? Who said that?' And waving his fists, stood up from his seat, 'I will break your bones!' The college boys were having a ball. They were laughing like mad. One of them barked again loudly, at which the old man let his lid fling off and he began shouting at the bus driver. STOP THE BUS! STOP THE DAMN BUS! I AM COMRADE! COMRADE SUKHANSAZ! STOP THE BLOODY BUS!

Oh the bus conductor really panicked. He was already glancing suspiciously at the racket throughout, now he thought some fight had broken out or something. He brought out his steel rod from under one of the front seats and came directly toward the old man and waving it toward him, he said, 'Babaji, why making noise haan? Where do you get off?'

'Show me some civility! I am a poet! People know me! They love me!'

The bus conductor was scratching his crotch, and seeing everyone laugh, relaxed a bit and said, 'Babaji, just don't make any noise. Take your seat,' he pointed the rod to an empty seat. 'Your stop is about to come.'

As soon as he finished saying this, someone shouted again from behind: *Oye Chicken-saz! You crazy old man!* Comrade turned to the students again, and having really lost it this time, began shouting, 'Fuckers! I have seen the likes of you many times! I have fought police with bare hands. I went to jail. Yes, jail! For eight years! People love me! Sisterfuckers! What do you know! I have given sacrifices for this country! I have fought against the exploiters, and you, you fuckers like you, don't care about anything!' Everyone in the bus was in fits. The conductor then came to him, 'Get off, babaji, your stop has come. Get to the gate, come on, come on hurry-up!'

As the old man moved towards the door, the boys kept up their chants:

Fight me Comrade!
Why are you scared, Comrade?
We also love you Comrade!
Comrade, you crazy old buffoon!
Another poem, Comrade, please?
Fight, Comrade! Fight!

He got off at Cantt Station, right at the end of it.

Yeah, just about ten minutes before the bomb blast. He was the closest person I knew who probably might have died there. Well, no, I don't know what happened after that. No, I have his cartoon though. Here.

To Live

I WAS SWEATING INSIDE my mother's car in that freak lane, saying to myself, 'Come on, come on,' while glancing in my rear-view mirror searching for her female figure to hurry along in my direction. All I saw was a man of densely hirsute armpits uncomfortably seated on a chair too small for his awesome behind and poking a scratching stick in the back of his vest. Right opposite him, a little left-over fire nibbled at the heap of burned garbage, excreting a rancid smell I knew well from memory.

It had been three minutes now and nothing had emerged from the corner of the lane. I hated every second of it. I tightly clasped the ignition key. You had to be prepared when waiting for a girl you've never really met before. I was in an old, clunky Suzuki FX, matchbox of a car—but I could've been off with it in less than three seconds, and on a bet, out of the lane in the next five, pedestrians and the incoming traffic notwithstanding. The car, if you want to call it that, was impossible to accelerate. But I had mastered that art as well—if you simply floored the gas pedal, no matter your timing with the gears and all, it steadied out at around 58 km per hour mark, often dwindling to 55. I knew how to jack it up to 77-type and keep it there.

All this was beyond my mother's maddest dream, of course, this car being her lifeline. She had put her savings into it—that she had brought with her when she divorced my father. She treated the car like her ringdove; I thought it my fighting dog. I wasn't allowed to touch this car, except in extraordinary circumstances. She was sleeping when I pushed the car to the end of the lane before igniting it and getting away. I had been waiting a long time to see this girl, Sapna. I had worked hard on her. I called her before leaving the house; she said she was ready. Planning inside my mother's sleep schedule, I gave myself an hour to get back.

It took me fifteen minutes to reach the spot where she was supposed to meet me. She had explained her location with the crookedness of someone who did not venture out of the house much. 'It is the second lane on your right, from the roundabout,' she had said. Wrong. It was the third. I was saved the frustration because she had mentioned, just as a by-the-way, 'Oh and you will see a metal-shiner's pushcart. You will see pots and pans. He just stands at the corner of my lane. That's how I remember it myself.' That's how anyone remembers anything in this city, where most streets don't have names.

I turned into the lane with the pushcart which was

neatly heaped with black pots, along with a smaller dump of grey, polished metalware. A man squatted on the pushcart, scrubbing a little pan. Her house was the third one on the left, the tiny white construction that occupied the tight space between two houses. For some reason, the house was named *Patang*, that is, Kite. I spotted it without trouble. I slowed down the car to notice any suggestions of her through the windows. I didn't see anything, except maybe a curtain move in the top room. But that could have been anything. I was supposed to take the first left into the first lane and wait outside an old yellow house with the black gate. She would come, she'd said, when she sees my battered blue FX pass by her house. That was the farthest she had come in showing her interest in meeting me in our one month of phone conversations—and I was happy for it. Well, girls are like that. At least at first. They need to taste blood for them to discover their hungers. She was a shy one and I was actually quite thrilled to meet her. Finally.

Frankly, no matter how many times you did it, it was always nerve-racking to meet a girl for the first time, especially if you've already had intimate conversations on the phone. She was convinced I was madly in love with her. I was seeking to cement that impression, among other, better things. She'd seen me, of course—and probably liked what she saw too. We went to the same place for our after-college private tuitions that I had quit after two classes because I'd much rather spend that money on something more useful.

I fancied her from the moment I walked into that drab tuition centre—dark, dusty, windowless room, lit with fifteen tubelights and furnished with secondhand chairs and desks from which nails poked out, and worse yet: full of mostly boys who spent their school time working their asses off and still came to tuitions for extra practice. Girls were too few, and perhaps that was the real reason why I left that place. She was pretty though. Wore a half-sleeved yellow kameez, had short hair that fell around her face when she bent forward to read, and she smiled all the time. Her deep square necklines made quite an impression on me and I studied her intently for the two sessions I was in the tuition centre. The second day she wore a khaadi-brown kameez with even shorter sleeves, and I scrutinized the back of her taut, fine neck for the whole hour and a half, and was left with no doubts I was going to try her. She was small and beautiful and perfectly packaged to be taken home and played with.

I found it a little difficult to find her number, but I managed after bribing the registration handlers of that tuition centre. I called her. 'I know you, and like you too. I just want to talk. Make friends.' It confused her at first—or at least that's how she made it look. It's true, most boys don't approach girls like that. They wait around, do idiotic things like passing snide remarks or acting loud and brash. She was suspicious at first, understandably, but then I gave her time, let her make the choices (at least that's how I made it look to her), left my number and told her she could call me if she wanted to. She did, of course. And the rest, as they say, is history of one month ago. She had many questions for me, many sadnesses of her own to report. She lived with her mother and a dying father (cancer, something like that) and her brother, who paid for them, and routinely threatened to turn them or himself out of the house. Anyway, after a point, I didn't care much about it. There wasn't much I could do. I was her only male contact and I broke her loneliness in a way that was new to her. In less than a month, she had fallen in love with me, she believed. And I with her. As I said, the latter was her own subjective judgment with which I did not interfere.

Well, that's what it's really all about if one thinks about it. Conversations. You want to be seen by others the way you see yourself. Boys think girls are looking for something that they could worship—and they go on adding weight to their six packs and nine biceps and so on, and all they ever end up doing is stand posing in busy markets. Jerks.

I took my eyes off the rear-view mirror—I'd had enough of the man in the lungi who seemed to have located the spot of his itch and was resolutely scraping it—and was checking the fuel tank indicator when the door opened abruptly and a figure wrapped in a shawl jumped inside. 'Let's go, let's go!' For a second, I couldn't move. But the next moment with the invasion of a perfume I was assured. She was prepared, I was happy to note. The car screeched a little and in less than five seconds, we were out of her freak lane and on the main road. She sat diagonally on the passenger seat, facing me. My first thought was, 'Do I look all right? I hope I'm not sweating.' Well, I was sweating. But so what, she loved me—and it was all right for a lover to sweat. She took off her shawl. I got a chance to look at her—and ah, that yawning neckline. She saw me looking at her and smiled. I smiled too.

My plan was to take her to an ice cream parlour with an empty second floor at that time of the afternoon. We could improvise something there. And besides, I had little money and that was all I could afford. But then, I was a little nervous myself, and didn't want to appear abrupt, so I kept silent. She didn't say anything and we drove quietly. Finally, after a while, I broke the silence, 'So, where should we go?' I asked.

She didn't reply for a few seconds. I was about to navigate her to my preferred spot, when she said, 'I don't know... I want to go somewhere far where we could talk.' Ah, yes. Talk.

At that moment, we had reached Shahrah-e Faisal, the jugular vein of the city, and I was still thinking of something funny to tell her to break up the tension. I put my FX in the fast lane and pumped the pedal to top up the speed. I could feel the exertions of the engine. She sat with her hands folded and I felt happy that she was wholly concentrated on looking at me. Suddenly she blurted, 'Why not go to the sea?'

Well, not a bad place to be but I knew it would be

impossible if I were to get back in an hour. After being kicked out of school, I had been my mother's prime cause of insomnia for the past two years. My communication with her had collapsed when I was expelled from the school. Things had improved lately since I had enrolled in an accounting degree diploma but there was no way I could explain this running away to her—with her car. I had already broken the excuse-bank of friendly accidents and flying donkeys trampling me in their descent from the heavens. I found it difficult to imagine how much further I could damage her and what that would look like—'Yes, that's what I was thinking as well,' I said to her. 'Okay, let's go. You have time right?' I was surprising myself. This girl had unanticipated effects on me.

'Haha!' I heard her crackle. 'Yes, yes. I can be out for another two hours. But not more, okay?'

I smiled but with a tightening in the chest. I had noticed the man intently staring at us from the car next to us. I didn't know what the hell was up with everyone in this city. Why must you face distrusting stares and smiles from everyone if you have a girl next to you in the car? But again, that depends upon your car: if you have a shiny, sexy four-wheel drive, you may well be screwing her in there and no one would dare take any notice—well, that's an exaggeration, but really. If you are in a little broken car, well, everyone will screw you as they cruise by. I stared back at the man who was staring at Sapna from the car window on my right.

Actually what really scared me about being on the road with a girl next to me were my own memories. When I was at school, we sprayed ink from our van window at passersby. We especially targeted old men, and young couples we suspected of doing wrong by meeting each other in private. You jerked off your ink pen when you were close enough—and pha! You stunned them if your ink-lasso caught them on their faces. They usually broke into curses. Young couples were most fun to target because they showed most reaction and could do least harm in return because they were tied up with each other and would not come after you. There were exceptions, of course. In that sense, I was afraid someone like me from my own past would leap out and do what I did, or something like it, like fling an egg at the windscreen.

I looked around and told Sapna, 'Roll up the window and lock the door.'

She seemed surprised, 'Why, what happened?' she paused for a reply.

'Well, because it's my car,' I said, suddenly irritated.

'I'm feeling hot,' she retorted and rolled it up by an inch.

I realized I probably sounded patronizing the way I ordered her. That act of hers of running away with me on a sore afternoon and the risk she took could have resulted in her limbs being broken by her parents if they found out. I knew she did this because, as she said, 'I want to do what I want to do—not what *they* want me to.' I had offended her sense of freedom. That act of being with a man (she loved) in a strange place was what she wanted to do. And I was happy for her, for my own reasons, of course. But I should've been more careful.

That little disagreement caused silence. I already felt a little annoyed watching everyone gawk at her—the beggars, newspaper boys, flower-sellers at traffic signals—and then the horrible traffic. I hated the rickshaws and motorcycles. And I had to get back home too.

At the Cantt Station stop, where the traffic was crawling because the buses clogged the turning and bus drivers took their pissing-breaks, I spotted Comrade Sukhansaz descending from a bus, almost falling out, actually. It scared the life out of me. He would report me to my father who might report me to my mother, which would destroy my access to this car and everything else. There was nowhere I could have gone—I was parked between the behind of a shiny black Civic and the front of another, and we were all standing there honking our heads off at each other. He stood in an aggressive posture, his fists clenched, looking at the bus that had dropped him off.

'Damn,' I said, craning my head out of the window to block at least some of our view of each other.

'What happened?'

'I think he's seen me.'

'Who has seen you?'

'That guy in the red cap. Oh damn. Don't look, don't look.'

'So?'

Well, there went my first impressions of being a brave, brave boy from a good, liberal family.

He had seen me, for sure, but I pretended I did not see him. We were moving inches. You fight for inches on this city's roads. You train your eyes to scour them and the rest of yourself to devour them. Drive to survive.

Fortunately, Comrade stood at a point after which the traffic smoothed out, and I raced past him. He had seen me for sure because he had his hand up, not as in stopping me, but waving to me.

We must have gone a couple of hundred metres and we were just starting to ascend the bridge on the left as soon as you cross the Cantt signal, when the blast occurred. Almost instantaneously something flew and smacked solidly into the back windscreen. The strength of the explosion was so terrible that for a second it shook the bridge we were on, and the car, which was already whining from its ascent up the bridge, lost power. Sapna's hands trembled and she turned around to watch the unforgiving spectacle unfolding behind us. 'Don't look,' I told her, as I pulled the handbrake to keep the car from sliding down the bridge.

The next few moments were vague and my hand fumbled with the keys and instead of turning it in the ignition, it seemed to be trying to understand it. I turned the key hard, shoving it inside the ignition. I anticipated the bridge would blow up next. My hands felt too weak and I was seething with anger. Why me? Why us? Why now? Why here? 'Duck!' I shouted at her. 'Hunh?' her eyes were stunned and glued behind us. The car came to life finally, but after what felt a long time. I dropped the handbrake and pumped the gas pedal so brutally the car squealed as it raced up the bridge.

Cars raced toward me from the other end of the bridge, wrong way. No one seemed to have any idea about the location of the blast and those idiots were just madly tearing toward the site itself. A Land Cruiser almost rammed into the car from the side. Bastard. One thing was clear: no one was going to stop. From there on drivers drove with their hands on their horns, cutting through the traffic lights and the traffic—everyone wanted to rush out from that centre of fire and hell behind them. Or toward it. They didn't care. Everyone wanted to be out of there.

I don't know how and at what speed I drove, but I drove faster than I ever did and it was not fast enough. Nothing felt safe or far enough. And when we emerged onto the sea, it was sudden, almost out of nowhere. I had been driving without registering anything at all.

The sea was deserted at that hour. It was on my right, but I was looking to my left, suspiciously at the apartments that stood stolidly, their dirty yellow paint dependably crumbling as always.

I parked the car, there was no one around. We kept sitting in there. I rolled down my window, and the breeze rushed in as if from another world, our hearts pounded like kicks in our chests, and the whole stretch of the sea seemed something new. It was not the desert it always seemed, not the deserted last bit of earth where I made out with other girls in the backseat of the car.

'Who was that man? The one in the red cap?' she asked.

'Comrade Sukhansaz.'

'What? Sukhan what? Is that even a name?'

'Well, he made it up. Sukhansaz is an Urdu word for poet. Comrade is what communists call each other—like, brother. This guy gave up his name for the cause, apparently. Spent years underground, in hiding. He was one of those few who didn't relent—didn't start an NGO or something like it.' I paused. 'I remember a few lines from one of his poems,' I said.

'*My lopped head will shout
My ripped tongue will roar*

'*Kill me, O bandits,
My death will be my beginning*'

I couldn't tell her the more obvious, more difficult thing: that the man was my grandfather. My father had a troubled relationship with him and had broken contact with him—much like I did with him when he and my mother separated. My mother says it was a blunder on her part to have married my father. A man who wasn't faithful to his own flesh-and-blood father could never be faithful to others.

'You think he died there?' she asked.

I did not reply. I was still quite deaf from the sound of the blast, and my hands were still trembling. I was thinking if I should tell her what flew to hit the back windscreen.

'Shall we get out?' I asked her.

We got out and leaned against the hot bonnet to face the sea. We did not make eye contact. Our hearts still pulsated with fear and our eyes were fiercely set on the sea. The sea breeze haggled in our ears. I felt her come close; the length of her arm touched the back of mine. Absurdly, there was a pink moon over the sky, looking like a faint dabble in broad sunlight. The migratory birds crisscrossed and flapped like a film reel in the air. We stood like that for a long time, breathing, and then, suddenly, she slid her cold hand into mine and held it tightly.

It wasn't until that moment I realized I needed comforting.

For the first time, in all my years of running here, I felt the sea in a new way. It did not seem like the end of the city.

Before setting off for home again, I went to examine the rear windscreen and found it as I feared: splattered with tiny bits of blood. I had clearly seen what it was that hit us. I wished I hadn't. I fought with my memory and tried to imagine it to be something else, but there was no time for that.

I cleaned the blood with a rag dipped in the car's radiator water. I found more splatters on the backlights, on the roof, the bumper. Sapna identified a couple of them on the door. I disposed of the bloodied cloth by flinging it on the road.

We couldn't afford to have anyone find out.

Lying Low

THE ENTRANCE DOOR SLAMS open and a new air kicks into the room.

You see one window rip-rooted from its welded joints and its steel edges poking through the net that is meant to bar mosquitoes. The slightest movement could slit the netting and send the panes crashing on the floor.

You should stand up and put the windows straight.

Your head hurts.

You'd fallen face-first on the floor.

Are you okay?

Your mother is moaning, 'Ya Allah, Ya Allah—,' her hand firmly pressed to her chest, as if trying to push her heart back into its original groove, 'Ya Allah, mercy—' her pain thronging in the final 'ah' of Allah. The other woman lying on the sofa is as mute as before. She had fallen unconscious a few minutes before the sound of the explosion tore through the room. You don't know what state she is in now.

You were wondering if you should take her to the hospital.

Yes.

Is she alive?

You must take her to the hospital.

But what if there is shooting outside? Yes, after a bomb blast there is shooting. Or another bomb blast. What about stray bullets?

You follow the slant of light cutting in from the broken window and stare at the ceiling to see where stray bullets would bore holes. Oh but wait—bullets smash through glass panes—'Get down! There could be stray—' you have an impulse to yell but you immediately realize that both women are too old to make abrupt moves. You feel a fizz in your spine. What must you do? Should you become their human shield?

You think of plugging the windows—you think sofas, pillows. You've heard that bullets do not pierce soft, woolly stuff but rip through hard surfaces like metal and wood and bones. But you immediately reject this idea as ridiculous because you don't have enough sofas in the house—in fact, just one, on which the two women behind you are seated right now. And besides even if you did have them, that would still entail going near the window.

You know it's not over—that you are in the middle of something; that something worse is sure to follow. You don't know what, but you can already taste its fear.

It tastes like a cold blunt knife in your mouth. It doesn't cut.

Worse is yet to come.

Lie low.

~

It was not a soft bald sound. It rammed through the window, kicked open the door and stabbed you between your shoulders. You went down face-first, as if by instinct.

Now your face is resting on the cold floor and you taste the dust you're breathing in through your mouth. Your mind flashes back to the other brush with death you had many years ago. Those last choking moments of consciousness flickering in your head before the grey/white water killed all lights.

You were five steps ahead of your friends, up to your shoulders in water and thinking of turning back, when your left foot skidded and the ground suddenly gave out beneath you and you tumbled forth, face-first into cold, salt-hard water. You kicked—water-in-your-nostrils, water-in-your-eyes, flailing, why-did-I-why-what-happened, your clothes water-logged, clawing you down, your friends shouting, pulling away from you against the grey/white saline water gouging into your eyes—to stay afloat but a few minutes of tossing and turning, water choked through your nostrils into your brain. You felt bloodlines beneath your shoulders, in your thighs, that hold you up, swell stiff. You couldn't move your arms any more. Your final effort was a powerful two-legged kick that threw you up an inch and then, down. A swipe of cool sudden grey/white darkness fell around your eyes.

You came to life with your head bouncing against a dirty red water cooler, your body ached, bruised all over. The waves had pulled you far into the sea and it was only luck/fate/God (you haven't decided yet) that had you saved. The two fishermen in vests on the farther end of a broken boat were making tea in a blackened pot on a kerosene-powered stove. They smiled when they saw you, asked you in their dialect, Are you okay, brother? Will you have some tea? Sit, brother. Your head must be hurting. Here, have some hot tea. It's okay. You will be fine. We are cooking some food. Where do you live? We'll be in Keemari by evening. Where do you live, brother? Oh you need to go to bathroom? No special room here for that. Piss on the sea that tried to kill you. Haha. Haha. You want some more tea, brother?

You sat at the edge of the boat and gawked at the great grey sea surrounding you. The air reeked of fish and kerosene. It was the most alive smell you'd ever smelled— the smell of survival. You threw up.

Your brain short-circuits into that fish-kerosene smell. You feel the same burning sensation in your neck, the sudden opening of sweaty pores. Yes, you feel that now. The same body-anger at being chosen to die. Once again something inside is protesting: Why you? Why? Why now? You have done nothing to deserve this. You shouldn't have to deal with this. There is something different though. Now you're sensing death not as a blank mortifying fear of you choking out of breath or your heart seizing up but now it feels more like a fear *for* something outside of yourself. The terror you feel now is of being cut out of something. You desperately wish to see your son and tell him you are fine. You want to hold his hand like the time when he was a ceaselessly crying newborn and you were alone in the hospital room sitting next to his cot feeling a kind of raging joy, an awe, as if you were looking at Life itself, a presence of something divinely *new*, as if you had just begun a life outside yourself, and nothing, not even death, could damage all your dying rotting parts that you felt each day. You listened to your son's crying for a while, waiting for his mother to return, but you couldn't take it after a while. You dipped the edge of a little white plastic spoon in honey and rubbed it against his lips. Sucking on it, he tightened his tiny grip around your little finger.

That's what you want now.

But here you are faced with two old, very old women who cared for you when you were too young to know what caring meant or how it is done—or if it is even necessary. At that point in your life, you were simply selfish: you wanted love but were incapable of giving any back.

You are still being selfish.

Would you be able to bear it in case the worse happens to them?

You feel trapped.

Your head's still hurting. You lie low.

~

Just twenty minutes ago you were watching your mother place an orange slice into Noor Begum's toothless mouth. She chewed the orange slice in her mouth until it was a thick lump of tasteless threads. She seemed to have lost the capacity to gulp down her food. You fell into thinking about her; how you found her at the airport, after years, and like this; she would have died in a garbage dump if you had been late. How did this happen? Her once luminous skin was now a wreckage of wrinkles; the wild-ivy of creases shrouded every inch of her face and hands.

As Noor Begum churned on the orange slice, your mother gave you a long, broken look. Clearly, she was shaken to see her this way too. Then she inserted her two fingers in Noor Begum's mouth, and surgically removed the lump swathed in gluey saliva. She asked you to get a glass of water from the kitchen. But in your mind you were trying to decipher the look your mother gave you. You knew what it meant: 'That's what happens when kids abandon their parents—' You felt she was accusing you for abandoning her and, perhaps, your father.

You felt angry.

You wanted to remind her who was in error. You

47

wanted to tell her that nothing you had done to her could ever match up to what she did by forgiving your father after how he punished both of you for years. That there was no graver offence than what happened last week when you found your father in this apartment—and you had turned around and slammed the door shut on his face and shot down the stairs. That just because you had not spoken to your mother since then did not mean that you were not enraged. Yes, you wanted to tell her how angry you'd felt at seeing your father in this apartment. Not only that. You wanted to remind her of all her mistakes: that accepting and supporting your father in his work was a mistake; and sticking with him was even worse. That while he went out and got drunk and recited poetry to a bunch of runaway charsis, she never stopped him—in fact, said, 'He cares for the world more than you or I or everybody who criticizes him'—that was a mistake. And now, after years of disappearance from your lives, now that his poetry and his fucking Communism and his revolution were dead and he was a raving old lunatic, to accept him back into her house now, to comfort him—*precisely* when it was right to leave him to himself for the way he punished both of you for years, YEARS—was her worst mistake of all.

You did not say this.

You just gave her an angry glance in return. It was the kind of glance that children give their parents when they know exactly the kind of total power they have over them and when the temptation to shatter them with one word, one phrase is overwhelming, but something—just the vague knowledge perhaps that the mess they create would be too great to gather—holds them back.

(Did your son ever give you this look? He didn't. He battered you with indifference instead.)

You got up to get water and that's when you caught sight of the skin of your mother's head through her hair. Her hair was now very thin; and oiled, they stuck on her head. All of a sudden you realized how old she was. You felt sorry for what you were thinking and for your hard, angry glance. Maybe she did not mean to accuse you with her look. Maybe she simply pitied Noor Begum and cared to share how she felt with you.

You brought her the glass of water and took your place against the window—a safe distance away from the workings of the two women. Your mother was sponging the orange juice coursing down the sides of her mouth. Your initial feelings of pity and disgust for Noor Begum had now subsided and you found yourself in some other, more liminal space between your childhood and the present. Now you felt sorrow for her. Deep sorrow. It reminded you of things.

~

Noor Begum lived in a house of dirty-pink walls toward the end of your lane. It was your neighbourhood before your father decided he had to be closer to the railway workers and you all moved to this apartment near Cantt Station, where now your mother lived alone.

You were eight then. On those hot, sticky afternoons, you walked through the front door of Noor Begum's house into the room where you and seven other kids assembled in a loose semi-circle to read the Qur'an. You all sat on a small worn-out green carpet at the centre of the room. It's fuzzy to think of it now: those afternoons next to the large window through which the sunlight sent in shadows with perfect edges now seemed suffused with a dull sense of mystery. You recited Arabic for an hour, and after reading for a while, descended into a lull, a dizzy drone. Your bottoms hurt from sitting on the ground.

You daydream about those slow afternoons in your chilly air-conditioned office in a shopping mall overlooking the sea. You even had a chapter about Noor Begum in the book you are writing about yourself, about your successful career, all about your humble beginnings and how you faced those challenges and rose to where you were now. Yes, you were a success. You owned the largest video game playland in the city. You had started small, in a rented shop under an apartment building. Now you owned an entire floor in the most upscale shopping mall in the city. You had a passion for games too. Even the title of your book, *Run*, was inspired from the video game, PacMan. The game embodied your ideals of living a successful life: Get the dots, avoid the ghosts, move up one level at a time. No shortcuts, no exits, and absolutely no pauses whatsoever. You believed in a relentless cutting down of the unnecessary—thoughts, imagination, ideas—which had been the reason of your success.

To be honest, you've been writing your book for an audience of one. You wanted your son to read the book because you knew he was a reader, or at least he was until two years ago. It'd been about two years since you last had a real conversation with your boy. He had refused to see you after your wife left you over your affair with the woman in the office. (To this day you do not know how your wife discovered. She had such precise details there was no point in arguing. You suspect that that bitch sleeping with you told your wife herself.) You had tried to explain to her that it did not *mean* anything to you. It was…just… *something*…without emotion or thought. It was *nothing* really. Nothing. But it was all over very quickly. She stepped out of your large luxurious house in Defense with her son and moved to a small apartment with an exorbitant rent on Tariq Road you were not allowed to visit. Your son, seventeen then, refused to see you afterward. She worked a job plus she had her savings of years with you—she had been smart that way—she kept her money separate from you. Your son was nineteen now. He drove his mother's battered little FX. You saw him last week outside the new McDonald's. He was visibly upset when you approached him. But your heart raced. He did not move when you put your arms around him. He had grown up radically in a few months. Broader shoulders, sharper eyes, more confident and aloof the way he stood. You felt his warmth, smelled the odour of his sweat. You wanted him to sit with you but he said he had to go. You were a little pushy but then you noticed the girl who was with him. You realized this probably wasn't the best time. So you said goodbye. You asked him to call you. Call you tonight. You will be waiting. Will you call? Yes. Good.

Needless to say, he didn't call. You waited, trying your best to explain to yourself his point of view; that he was hurt; that anybody who had gone through the same would do the same.

That was your life now that you did not understand. And you started to write out of a desperation because you felt this might help you make sense of your life. Also, because evenings had become unbearable. And you wanted your son to know. You wanted him to *know* you. Learn from your experience—there was so much you wanted to share. Ask you questions. Say, Wow, Baba. You are the best.

So you wrote about your life and Noor Begum and things and their reasons.

You suffered a bout of nostalgia while writing the chapter on Noor Begum. You wanted to write about the awkward squats as you sat loudly reciting the Qur'an, say how your foot felt grinded from bearing all your weight while sitting on the floor, the rapid *tak-tak* of the ceiling fan as it spun the air with its dusty blades, the dizziness...But you wrote: 'Noor Begum's house provided the comfortable environment for Qur'an lessons and my early lessons in disciplining myself into working through boredom.' Yes, instead of writing what you *felt*, you wrote about *lessons* about disciplining yourself—but really, you knew that lessons are derived only afterward. Discipline was something you admired only in theory. Your life and success were not a result of discipline, rather a series of smart choices and knowing what to do when opportunities present themselves. You were a big believer that every person, no matter how poor or unfortunate, gets at least *one* shot at a breakthrough in life. But you wrote about discipline regardless because, well, you did not want your son to get the wrong idea. You didn't want him to misinterpret your words and see you as an *opportunist*, which he probably did already.

That was the strange problem with writing, you had discovered. Meaning never matched the words, and words always evaded the thought. Before you had started writing, you could picture the clean arcs of your life. You had clear ideas. But what finally made it onto paper was circular and loopy and joined at the wrong ends with everything else. It messed up the whole picture. So you abstained from saying too much. You described Noor Begum as the 'perfect teacher who never fell ill' and moved on. You didn't say anything about her small, healthy, luminous face, her extraordinary almond eyes filled with dark pupils, her glowing skin, wheaty complexion, her thin lips, her calmness as she sat with a bowl on her lap and heard you all read aloud.

You wanted the whole thing matter-of-fact; you despised the poetic. Poetry, all of it, reeked of the kind of idealism your father embodied. You were everything because of your father: he was your model of what not to be. You'd learned your contempt of idealism, of poetry, of philosophizing from him. You believed in the two-dimensional simplicity of PacMan. The clarity of where to go and what to avoid available at all times.

You've expressed your views on poetry and poets in your book in no uncertain terms. 'Poets,' you've written, 'are hungry and curious creatures—but only about what's inside them. And the only way they usually know to get there is by tearing themselves up at the seams. They are always scattered inside. They only know how to tear themselves up.' These were the most poetic lines in your book, and needless to say, they were inflicted on your father.

～

Your Qur'an classes were a conspiracy between you and your mother. Your father would not have tolerated it. He considered religion mixing up with everything the cause of all problems in this God-forsaken country.

He did not, in fact, tolerate it when he found out.

It happened one day when he came home early and caught you on the stairway with the Holy Book in its crimson silk envelope edged with golden embroidery and the rehl, its wooden stand, in your hand. He was puzzled at first. He asked you, 'Where are you coming from, what is this'—but then he saw the white cap on your head and squinted his eyes. He calmly took the cloth envelope from under your arm and opened it. '*This*? Where—? For how long?' You were about to say something but you stopped. His face had started to tremble. He climbed up the stairs ahead of you and banged the door of your apartment. He was yelling out your mother's name telling her to open the door. The door did not open and he finally had to fumble the key out from his own pocket. When he entered, your mother was rushing out of the bathroom, water splashed around the neck of her kameez.

'Is THIS what you have been teaching my son? *This*?' he hissed. 'You want to fill his brain with *this*? *What* do you want him to become?'—and then he exploded: 'I ALWAYS KNEW YOU. I KNOW YOUR KIND. YOU WITCH. YOU WANT TO TAKE MY SON AWAY FROM ME. I WILL KILL YOU. THINGS YOU HAVE BEEN TEACHING MY CHILD. YOU WANT TO STEAL HIM. I KNOW IT. I ALWAYS KNEW IT. I WILL KILL YOU.'

It was the one time in her life that your mother did not back down. She raised her voice to match his—'I will teach him what I think is best for him. He is my son first. Look at yourself—you want him to be like you? You think you are a role model for my son? Haan?' He grabbed plates and glasses with both his hands from the table and hurled them at her feet. Shaken, terrified, she stood with her back against the kitchen door guarding her other things she had collected out of her savings, and kept answering back. You felt your father might hit her or throw her out of the house—as he was threatening her. You quietly moved to grab your mother's wallet and dupatta in case it happened.

Then the doorbell rang. And both of them fell silent.

~

There's an echo of that mortifying silence thirty years ago in this room rocked by the bomb blast. How you had hated your father afterward as you watched your mother sweep the broken glass off the floor intermittently stopping to control her tears. Now with one-half of your face sweating against the floor, you feel a surge of sympathy for your mother. And the same deep hate for your father.

Oh, he was about to visit you! You had forgotten! Your mother had told you when you came into the apartment with Noor Begum. She didn't try to hide her bitterness, 'I am telling you so I won't have to hear anything later. It's up to you if you want to stay.'

There was no need for her to say that. She said it precisely to ask you to stay. She wanted you to reconcile with your father. You had yelled at her countless times, but she persisted. 'My son, you need to be good to your father. He's your father after all. He's made mistakes but he's an old man. He's so weak even…mentally…My son, even God forgives. Who are we to hold grudges?'

'Then let God forgive him,' you gave her a curt reply.

But there's no escaping this now: if he comes into the apartment now, right now, and finds you like this, and says, Hello, son, what would you say?

～

You don't want to think of your father. You don't ever think about him—you have trained your mind to think away from him, to other things big, small, meaningful, meaningless. In your book you talked about his life in more general terms. His life is used as a symbol for irresponsible living. As a person, you do not discuss him in any detail: you've given him a nondescript life, 'someone with communist leanings' and you never mention him again.

Your father was a communist poet, for whom family was largely an inconvenience. When you were twelve, he'd decided to separate himself from his family to commit himself to the revolutionary cause. So he disappeared. Later, he went into hiding for being a Left-wing political activist; he quit journalism and took up carpentry. But he remained active in organizing workers and protests and wrote poetry.

All these years, you resented your father for his selfishness and for the suffering he inflicted on you and your mother for his idealism. Practical men, contrary to the idealists' bias, are the least selfish: they even use selfishness to benefit their families and country. Artists, poets, writers—idealists, all sorts—hide their selfishness in the garb of philanthropy and they end up doing more harm than good—to everyone, most of all their own selves and families. They are weak men who destroy others. Your father was a weak man.

But when you were writing about your father in your book, you found yourself veering from this idea of your father's life. Your memory haemorrhaged into images and incidents that you thought never happened. You found yourself sleepwalking through secret doors, segueing into things that didn't fit the two-dimensions of your life, falling through holes that led into vast halls of greater darkness.

When writing the story of your life, you, for instance, remembered that your father did not abandon you entirely. He used to come pick you up from the house—even during his days of hiding. He'd take you to his new place outside the city, where he worked as a carpenter. You started remembering, and then, without realizing, started writing about those afternoons: Your father camped on his knees, vigorously planing a block of wood. Bent over, one hand clamped on the wooden block and the other firmly pushing the planer over its surface. The pedestal fan behind his sweat-drenched back lying dead. The recursive sound of the planer scraping wood echoing through the room with his hard, cavernous breathing. The room feeling like a grimy pool of heat.

He worked in that hard, resolute manner till his bushy brows were completely soaked with sweat; he then paused, put aside the planer, took off his large square spectacles, tilted his head sideways and wiped his brows with his finger. Sweat poured down his temples in a sudden stream and rapped the straw mat that he was squatting upon. He then walked up to the dirty orange water cooler which had a dripping ice block piled on top of it and filled a big steel cup with water and drank it in slow gulps.

You wrote this and remembered more. You remembered the nights too.

You were pressing his legs, with your little hands. You realized how his legs had grown thin, and he heaved loud and sibilant sighs when your fingers pressed into his calf-muscles, which were stiff and knotty. After a while, your wrists began to ache and you asked, 'Baba, should I stop?' He did not reply, so you covered his feet with the bedsheet and were about to get up when he said in his wispy, shredded voice, 'You must say to yourself, "What a father. What a *fucking* father".'

For a minute, it was as if a flash exploded in your face. You did not move. It was too dark to see his face, but you were certain that a tear was shuffling down his cheek. You took his cold, sweaty hand in yours and held it awkwardly. And obviously, it brought no relief to either of you. You were trying to console him, but even then you knew he was right. You did hate him for loving his revolution more than you and your mother. It was impossible to give him any consolation, so you just sat there quietly on his bed, listening to the bleached silence between both of you, collecting the frothy sounds of the passing cars.

A few seconds later, he lapsed into mumbling angrily to himself. His eyes were aflutter, his head moved as if trying to encircle his escaping thoughts. Every few seconds he sucked in the air with a loud sibilance. 'Yes, yes,' he'd say in his scratchy voice, and then lapse back into, 'Hmm, hmm,' as if agreeing with somebody absent. When you drew out your hand from his, you realized that he was not holding it at all.

These were pages that didn't make it into your book but they all return to you jostling and clambering for space in the story of your life now as you're lying chest down, shoulders down watching a cloud of dust billowing into the room through the empty window socket.

This suddenly feels much worse than the terror you've felt.

Or is it another face of the same fear?

~

Listen: you look ridiculous, lying on your belly holding your breath like a lizard stuck on the ground darting its eyes both ways.

You cautiously rise to your knees and walk up to the windows that are poking at the netting. Without touching anything, you peep through the side of a window and see a lot of fire and dispersing men. From five storeys above, you can discern a clear circumference of explosion. You quickly run your eyes, looking for guns, for somebody sitting in a sniper's position—and find nothing. Everything is scratched and seared. Buildings like live charcoals. Smoke in hot black clouds. Tar and scrapes of fire.

But now, so close to death, your mind is suddenly thinking about what you had written and discarded. You realize that you have suddenly become conscious of wounds you carried but could not see. Now looking out this broken window at people rushing toward sources of smoke, throwing water over burning cars and buses, you realize that what you had felt for your father was much worse than hate: it was a kind of love where it's impossible to know what you want, and where every act of reaching out lacerates you more deeply, and expression is impossible because no matter how hard you try you'll inevitably fall at odd angles to each other's needs.

Perhaps your son feels the same way about you.

And now you look at Noor Begum and realize you have no language to describe what you feel. No way to say how it wounds you to see her this way. Now, standing here, it is clear as day: more than anything else, you want to find words for what you feel and think and everything that is dark. And then this terrifying thought hits you: Yes, your father wrote poetry to find a language for his wounds. Yes, you in your own way have become your father.

People are still pouring in towards cars and buses that stand blasted out of shape. Should you go downstairs and try to help? You see a car toppled over, as if it had stepped on the bomb and was flung up in the air. A man tears away from another burning car with a large scrap of metal sunk into the back of his shoulder. He's screaming but his screams barely reach you. There is noise. People are shouting pointing to roasted bodies, skulls pierced with bits of shrapnel—soft and musty with blood. You pull away from the window with the image of a man squatting on the ground, holding his head.

You recall your car was parked close to the building. You must go down to examine the damage.

You ask your mother if she's okay. If Noor Begum's okay? She's still moaning, 'Hai, hai Allah, hai Allah...' Your eyes pause over the gentle throb of the jugular in Noor Begum's neck, the raisin skin of her neck. She's still alive. But is she well?

You ask her to move to the other room with Noor Begum, which would cordon you from the worst, if it comes to it. You lift Noor Begum's papery body in your arms. Her face still doesn't seem to register anything. She stays numb and your mother gently lifts her dangling arm and wraps it around your neck. All of you move to the other room behind this one.

Noor Begum's clothes (white shalwar kameez, tiny roses) stink. You think of the security guard at the airport who was pushing her. You had recognized her voice as she hit the security guard's chest with her fists telling him, 'Let me go to Mecca, son, let me go to Mecca. I have been summoned, my son, let me go there. I have no one here, let me go.' The guard was speaking over the walkie-talkie, 'Yes, there's another one. Come get her. I am on duty.' You approached the woman and realized it was Noor Begum. 'Is this your mother?' the guard asked rudely. You shook your head and told him you knew her, to which he said, 'You know where she lives? Then take her away if you can. Otherwise these airport people will leave her somewhere on the highway and she might get hurt. Take her if you can.' What did he mean by leaving her on the highway, you asked. 'O Sir-ji, these old senile people show up at the airports asking to be sent to Mecca for Hajj, or to their children or relatives who have moved to other countries. They don't know their addresses or anything else, so we put them in our car and leave them far away. They are a nuisance. Amma, get away from me...' he pushed her again. There was no point in taking Noor Begum to your own house. There was nobody there.

You think about how you're going to write about this incident in your book. Your father should be here any minute—wait where was he...

That moment you hear an almighty crash. You dash into the room and see the glass panes in a huge mess on the floor. The netting ripped and tattered.

Your book needs to be rewritten.

The door is still open.

Your Wounds Are Your Eyes

Ever seen a bullet-smashed windscreen?

The hole at the centre becomes an eye. You see less through it but you gain focus, sharpness. That's how it is—our wounds become our eyes. Seeing outside becomes seeing inside.

Listen.

A WRITER IN THE CITY

The Truants

THE COLOURFUL TASSELS HANGING from the ceiling bobbed above the bus driver's head, the floral patterns flowing along the window panels turned into spirals and whorls and peacock feathers and feminine eyes, and the feisty colours of the ceiling—orange, blue, red and turquoise... It had been four years since I had been on a bus and it was a sudden raging blaze of memory.

I had not been on a bus since my father's death four years ago, and it all came back in a rush: the noise and the clatter, the staring men and vexed faces. The fear and frenzy I was ridden with a minute ago—of having run away from school, of the possibility of having been spotted while scaling the wall, of not even knowing the bus routes to the sea—were replaced with a sudden, strange feeling, and I looked around the bus like a near-blind man straining to see in dim light. Just then, a hand prodded me, 'What are you doing? Move!' Sadeq was trying to get in the bus and I was blocking the doorway. I took the seat on the right, next to the window. He came and sat next to me.

'Are you sure no one saw you when you climbed up the wall after me?' I asked him. He was rolling up his sleeves in even folds.

He dropped his sleeve abruptly and grabbed my face with both hands, 'Nothing has happened! No one has seen us! Understand? No one!' He dropped my face and resumed folding his sleeves. A silence fell between us and I felt my ears heat up.

The last kid who was caught bunking was caned in the school ground and then was left kneeling in the sun for the rest of the day. When he fainted from dehydration, his parents were called in and were humiliated in a parent–teacher conference, after which the boy was packed off with a one-month suspension certificate. I was sick with worry. My mother and I lived with my sister at her husband's house, who also paid my school fee. He was a cloth wholesaler, a charitable man who staunchly believed in helping his relatives. He believed their well-being was a reflection on his person, and he never failed to have a low opinion of those who were well-off but did not help their extended families. He had taken my mother and me into his house when my father died. But he was also a violently unpleasant man. He did not mind cursing his wife when angry. That very morning I had heard him yell through his bedroom wall, 'I will cut your throat, you hear! Don't you ever take money from the cupboard without telling me. I'll leave you out on the road! That's not your property. They are *savings*, SAVINGS! Bitch!' My sister emerged from the bedroom and went straight into the storeroom where she cried. My mother had left early for her job at the hospital and I was leaving for school.

Now that I had run away, I was trying to suppress the fear of what would happen if he found out that I have been bunking school that he paid for with his money. I would be lifted from the school and made to roll cloth at one of his shops, and my mother and sister would bear his wrath for being ungrateful.

Sadeq was annoyed at my questioning. He wasn't used to such company. I was trying hard to be as tough as him. Just before getting on the bus I had asked him what if we got suspended from school? He replied without even thinking, 'I don't know, why are you even thinking all this? We are *not* going to be caught. And oh, so what if someone has even seen us? What are you going to do about it now?' He tapped my cheek and said, 'Think positively, my dear.'

To be honest, I did not even know why I was running away. I thought of it as a natural progression of the recent changes in my person. I was never a shy or timid boy, but recently I had turned a swashbuckler. I'd learned how to bludgeon boys' egos, how to cut through their fathers, mothers and sisters, and wipe walls with their blood. The eager audience of my classmates, I found, were ever-ready, ever-present to cheer and jeer at my victims. And frankly, there were very few who could withstand my blitzkrieg of abuses, cuss words and filthy anecdotes about their mothers and sisters and bloody pimping fathers that I conjured and launched in just a few half-seconds.

My improvised witticisms were in Urdu, most of them very dirty, usually ending in and around the anus (it was an all-boys school). I had mastered the art to such a degree that I could reduce even the most unsuspecting, sheepish boys to a violent desperation. I did not stand down until I gained complete submission—annihilation, if you may—which usually ended in my prey's attempts to hit me (clumsy slaps, punch in the belly; but I usually got them before they could; grabbed them by their neck, most of them froze; if they didn't, then I'd bring them down—boys immediately realize their place if they look up at you from down below; if someone threw a hapless hand or foot my way, a kick in the gut set him right); but in most cases they'd simply let out despairing expletives that fell on laughing boys' ears. I was caught a few times: a punch on my ear and it bled; I was slapped this other time, again on my right ear and it whistled all night, the guy who hit me was a lefty. Bastard. The fucker even scratched my face. I think he was going for the eye, but Sadeq belted his arms from the waist and yanked him out just in time.

I was saved almost always by Sadeq's interventions.

Sadeq was someone I would have never befriended in ordinary circumstances: he hung out with the senior crowd of the school who smoked cigarettes and bunked classes—but he was the only one who had an answer to the darkness that had taken root in me after Baba's death. With him around, I felt a crack of light in my darkness.

I can't say I felt happy around him, just more secure. He regularly thumped my back and said things like, 'Don't worry, it'll be fine, just don't think about it,' without even asking what bothered me. He didn't wish to know. It was like that with him—he was not interested in emotional conversations. He was interested in people who could kick ass. And we were friends because I could: not with my fists but with my words. When it was just the two of us, he was interested in jokes. In fact, that's what our friendship was founded on—I told him jokes, the general rule being the dirtier the joke, the better. We had started bunking classes about a month ago, and when he evolved the bunk into an escape from the school, I took the plunge to prove I could do it—and here we were.

I looked around the bus and inspected the two kids with garbage sacks full of plastic bottles. They were stinking up the whole bus. My father would have struck up a conversation with them, asked their ages and places of residence, switched to their ethnic language and made them smile and instructed them that they should go to the evening school his friend ran for children who were working...

It wasn't nostalgia I felt, it wasn't even longing, it was something more immediate, a kind of stumbling encounter with someone too important to be forgotten but who had been forgotten nonetheless and was now leaning his weight on the door I had closed.

I felt a hurtling through my chest, a sudden rush of

blood in my fingers—I was feeling weak and ambivalent. I put my head on my suitcase-like schoolbag and imagined him. He seemed far away, like a man in some story and I was with him, the character who was now breaking away from the narrative to dream his own dream.

~

I am holding his finger and we are wading through the rush of the Empress Market. My hand is sweaty and I fear that it might slip. We are dressed in identical clothes; I am his micro-copy, both of us are in white kurta-shalwar, straddling the mass of men. I am continually falling behind him—and holding his finger is only a tenuous connection: as if his finger would break in my hand and he'd walk off without even noticing. He walks oblivious of his own body; his hands look like lifeless lumps hanging from the beam of his shoulders. After walking for a while, I have only a vague sense of him; it is just his sweat-streaked white kurta that assures me of his presence as I follow him.

We break into a less crowded area. He's trailing a chant: 'Po-etry, hist-ery, pheel-aasaphy, diee-gest, fayy-shion, booooks, all kinds, booooks, booooks!' It's cloudy and pleasant but very humid and we are both sweating. He pauses abruptly, the finger I am holding feels stiffer: his eyes are set on something in the distance and his lower lip trembles. It means he is angry. I realize what he's glaring at, but before I get a chance to distract him, he says, 'Look, just look at the filthy bastard.' He is pointing to the man who is squatting and pissing on a wall in a corner.

He loves the city and fully exercises his right to hate the transgressors who don't love it as much as he does: I watch him as he lets his anger burn through him. It short-circuits him into one of his spiels about the Islamization of this country during the Zia regime and how they removed public toilets and urinals, believing them to be an unIslamic way of pissing. 'Now you have bastards like these who piss all over the city...' he pauses and keeps staring. 'So much for Islam improving us.' I tug at his finger to bump his mind again into the chant, 'Po-etry, hist-ery, pheel-aasaphy...'

We make our way to the pushcart selling books. The bookseller's face lights up upon seeing him. He shakes off my grip from his finger and embraces the bookseller's hand. He then sifts through the stacks of books presented to him. I stand there bored while he has a chat with the bookseller about books, asking what-happened-to-that-one-I-asked-for type of questions. I'm not interested in books. I am still watching the filthy bastard who is now inserting a stone in his shalwar to dry the splattered piss-drops on his thighs and whereabouts. I feel a similar kind of hatred that my father channelled earlier—although I don't really understand my reasons for feeling angry.

Finally, my father's done. He hands me a white plastic bag with a few books and we enter the crowd once again. 'Baba, where are we going?' I ask.

He smiles. 'I'll teach you how to love the city, my son.'

I keep pausing and stretching out my other hand to keep people and their knees from bumping into me.

Sadeq tapped me on the shoulder, 'Oye, want to have a coconut?' I nodded and looked through the window to the road where a coconut hawker stood between two cars at the traffic signal. He was refreshing his sliced crescents, decorated in a flower-arrangement, by splashing them with water using a steel glass.

'How much?' I asked, sliding my hand in my pocket to draw out the money.

'Don't worry about the money,' he said, going to the window seat across from his. I didn't understand and watched him assume a position like a jaguar waiting for prey: his hands on the window bar, his eyes fixed on the coconut seller scurrying nearer to our bus in search of potential customers. He waited, waited, and just as the coconut seller went past him under the window, his hand snapped downward and pinched a slice that was lying loose in the puddle of water on the tray. He immediately leapt back across the aisle onto his seat.

He looked at me with lit up eyes, lifting the coconut slice caught in between his thumb and finger, 'Yes!' He lifted his other hand for a high-five. He broke the slice into two and I took the half he offered me. The taste of the scrubby-sweet-watery texture filled my mouth.

'It's just two rupees,' I said, trying to make my point casually. 'Why take the risk?'

'Abay, it is not about two rupees or five rupees,' he said looking at me, his face still red with triumph. 'It's about practising,' he smiled.

'Practising?' I was puzzled.

'Yes, if you're going to get anywhere in this place, you must protect yourself from getting fucked, and the moment you get a chance, you must fuck the other person. You understand? That takes practice. Learn the lesson early,' he said exultantly, chucking the last bite of coconut into his mouth.

The bus started moving. I looked out the window and caught a glimpse of the coconut-seller rearranging the slices on the tray. I felt a sting: he seemed to be counting for the missing slice.

Right then, I realized Sadeq was conversing with an odd-shaped head wiggling in front of him. 'My knee, you know, I cannot sit on that seat,' it was saying to him. 'Can I sit here, please hunh? You can take my seat, it's right here, just behind this one, hunh?'

Sadeq made a face and moved to the seat behind ours. A short, crooked man in a light crumpled red-checked shirt appeared beside me. His head was sparsely haired and defined like an overgrown bulb which was screwed with a tiny mouth. He had no teeth on the upper level, and the ones below, which he used for smiling continuously, jutted out in a constant display. I noticed the top buttons of his shirt were loose, and revealed the crinkly skin of his chest.

He smiled looking at me as I ate the last bit of my coconut. I nodded and turned to look out of the window. He tapped me on the shoulder and pointed to the red checks on my bag, 'Your bag matches my shirt—huee huee!' he said, looking amused.

I smiled and looked away again.

He paused and then leaned closer to whisper in my ear, 'Run from school, eh?'

Before I could reply, I heard his sniggering laughter, 'Huee hueee huee! I used to do the same… run from school. In fact, I ran away from college then from work. And now I am retired, I run away from my home!'

I was unsure about how to react to this information. He continued, 'You know, I don't go home for days because I like it here in the city—around all the noise and people.'

'Hmm…' I nodded.

'You know what I do around here?' he said somewhat triumphantly, after a thoughtful pause. 'Guess?'

I looked at him completely puzzled. 'I don't know?'

'Huee huee… I look for others who have run away and I write their stories. I am a *writer*.' He said with emphasis and looked at me with a delighted expression. His abundant glee disturbed me and I think he detected my discomfort. He immediately added, 'All of it completely imaginary, of course.'

'Hmm…' I said.

'Here, shake my hand,' he said. 'You are my friend now.' He pushed his hand forward. I looked at it, and reluctantly gave him mine. He snapped it. His jaw jutted out, and through his open mouth, I saw the broken architecture of his teeth. He had a surprisingly powerful grip. 'You see the power in this hand?' he said, his face glowing. 'You know how old I am?'

My hand was hurting. I looked around to see Sadeq. He had dozed off on his seat. 'No,' I said, trying to pull away my hand. It struck me how large his hands actually were.

'Guess?'

'Eighty-three!' I blurted out of sheer pain.

'Yes! Eighty-three! I turned eighty-three yesterday! See I told you people who run away are friends!' he released my hand. I felt the crushing pain in my hand but I didn't look at it. 'I will write your story now,' he said. 'Where are you going?'

'To the sea?' I said reluctantly.

'Haha! That's where they all go when they run away at first! But then they all come back. The sea, you see, feels good for only a few days, but then it starts suffocating you. You first escape to the sea to escape yourself, but after a while that's all you find there. City is better that way. There are too many lanes and alleys. You never run into yourself there.' Then he leaned closer and said again in a whisper, 'I spend my day in a café at Cantt Station. It has delicious fruit cake: cheap. Chai, so strong. Omelette, very reasonable rate. That's where you should come as well after you're tired of the sea. Okay? Look for me. I am there. *Writer*.'

'And yes, don't let them confuse you—,' he said, still smiling, as if reassuring me of something he thought I was afraid of. 'They will tell you all kinds of things, *philosophies*—huee huee—like I am doing now—huee huee! But that is all bogus stuff. All this philosophy business is bogus—even mine, huee huee huee...it's all meant to trap. Don't listen to anyone. Just keep running away...'

He went on for some time but I stopped paying attention to what he was saying. Something about him disturbed me, something about the way he spoke about the city. He got off with us at the Cantt Station and pointed me to the café he was talking about. He made the handshaking joke with Sadeq too; he was unable to guess his age.

While we were waiting for the next bus to the sea, we watched the old man hobble along the sidewalk. He was cripplingly old and permanently bent. He waved to a select few faces as he went along the sidewalk—the cobbler, the paan-seller, the little boy carrying tea, all of them stopped their work to exchange a word with him. He balanced himself by holding their shoulders. A little boy jumped when he pressed his hand. I heard his 'Huee huee huee!' in my head.

'What a jerk! The bugger has totally lost it with age, eh?' Sadeq said, smiling. I didn't like that but I kept quiet.

We got on the bus. I felt my father's presence once again.

It seemed to me he was there even when the old man was around, listening to him talk about his city.

'What was the bugger saying to you?' Sadeq asked as we seated ourselves in the bus again.

'Nothing, he was just proving to me how retarded he was. Telling me his adventures with whores.'

'What! Whores! Are you serious?' he jumped.

'Yeah. He even told me about a whorehouse near here, just behind some café. He said he was going there. He offered to fix us with some for cheap rates if we wanted. He said he was a pimp.'

'Oh yeah? Then why didn't he tell *me* that? Old bastard! But we should go! We should be careful. That's how they lure boys and then fuck them, ya? He looked like a bastard to me. I could tell by the way he pressed my hand. *Bhen ka*. It still hurts.'

'Yeah, but we should visit him sometime. He said he hangs out in that café.'

'Haha, yes, yes. But I didn't know you were into this stuff.'

'I'm not. But I think it's about time I should start getting into this stuff, no?'

'Haha, yes yes. Why not. We could start together. I have a couple of reliable links. You know, whores are shady people. You have to be careful. They have contacts with the police and ministers. They cut your dick if you mess with them. Be careful. That's what I've heard from friends.'

There was a pause. 'Oh, so I was thinking,' he smiled,

'about that joke you told me a few days back—the lion one, what was it? Tell it to me again. It was really funny, that one. I want to memorize it for my friends.'

'Haha, not now,' I said.

'What do you mean not now?'

'I mean I don't feel like it?'

'Abay you fucked up? Why not?'

I looked him in the eye; I knew he'd be sore if I refused—but I really didn't want to talk about it, especially because I wasn't feeling good. The old man was nice to me—I shouldn't have said all that about him.

I wanted to refuse, but then I just decided to get over with it quickly. The joke went something like this:

Once upon a time a fox goes outside a lion's lair and starts swearing at the lion who is sleeping inside: 'Oh fuck you, you cur! If you have any shame, come out and get me! Who's made you the king, you whore! Hey bastard, come now!' The lion glances at the fox with one eye still closed and turns over and continues sleeping. The fox continues to swear at the lion, and then even goes on to challenge his manhood. The lioness, who is witnessing all this, is outraged: 'What kind of a lion are you? Go get this half-breed of a fox, otherwise I'll have to do something!' When the lion ignores her as well, the lioness roars and runs after the fox. The fox dodges her and leads her into a hole in a tree trunk, through which the fox slips but the lioness gets stuck because of her bigger behind. The fox comes around and does a job on her backside—and disappears happily. When she finally returns to the den, she finds her husband angrily pacing up and down. He bursts out the moment he sees her, 'Are you happy now? Why do you think I was so sleepy? I was fucked five times last night!'

Sadeq laughed hard ('Hahaha! Five times! Fox! Hahaha!'). I turned away to look out the window.

~

We are sitting on a footpath, facing the Empress Market bustle and sharing a glass of lemonade from the pushcart. Before us, the perennial Empress Market traffic jam: cars, rickshaws locked behind buses on the narrow strip of road and the buses, gurring their engines as they wait for their seats to fill up before taking off.

My head feels hot and my tears are drying on my face. The slipper on my foot seems a dead, dust-ridden animal with a broken strap and mauled face.

It happened very quickly: I tripped and fell while trying to keep up with his pace. My slipper got lost under hundreds of feet. He had turned immediately and lifted me up, 'Are you okay?' he asked in a worried tone. I told him to find my slipper, which he did. But without realizing, I was crying—my palms and elbows were scratched with blood and dust, the skin grazed and burning. Soft drinks are a luxury my father cannot afford, but I am a crying child, so he takes me to the lemonade pushcart. He watches me with a smile while I slurp it up. I ask him, 'Baba, aren't you thirsty?' He shakes his head. I forcefully give him a sip. He takes a sip and returns it to me. He's a storyteller and he's looking at the buildings, as if daydreaming what it's like to be inside. He has receded into his recollection mood. He points me to the blue Konica one-hour photo board in front of us. 'When I was in college, instead of that, there was a horse-riding cap store. This place was the heart of the city, cleanest in all of the city. The most chic crowd came here. That building you see there was a billiard room. Expensive stuff. We couldn't go there on our student budget. That corner store, which is selling cheap socks, was a cabaret and a bar. But come.' He gets up and we walk.

He walks the streets with his arms spread wide, his chin cocked up. He walks as if he owns the city. We dodge a few pushcarts and he pauses to let a man complete spitting his phlegm in front of him. He stares at the man, who does not pay any attention to him. I pull him on and we then run to cross the road to reach the sidewalk of a park where the air turns into an incredible stench of piss. He points me to the building in front of us, which is a crumbling colonial façade on top and a camera store below. 'That was the India Coffee House,' he says. 'All the intellectuals, poets, and artists came there. You remember the sketches I have at home? All of them were made by my friend Salahuddin over a cup of tea. Everyone I met, everything I know about life and politics, I learned from there. I came here with my friends after college, which was near—the old Karachi University campus,' he takes a pause to laugh. 'The owner of that place used to shout when he looked at me: *Ho ho! Here he comes, our young intell-kachool!*'

I look at his smiling face and then turn to look at the decrepit old building and try to reconcile the emotion. It is then, perhaps, for the first time I am confronted with the fact that places and people are like things: both made of memories and meaningful to us in the same way: we construct ourselves in our conversations with them.

I am perhaps too young to realize all this, but my relationship with the city has already been established. It is one of perpetual loss.

Sadeq and I sat on the ledge facing the sea, our shirts filled with the gusty breeze. Our frenzied excitement upon first seeing the sea had subsided, and now we were flicking roasted chickpeas into our mouths. We were calm and without the need to speak with each other.

The sea at 11.00am in the morning was one Karachi dream that came true each day. It was one part of the city that remained as it ever was: a vast desert of water meeting a uniform spread of grey sand that shimmered with litter in sunlight: plastic bags lolled their heads in the constant

wind, half-buried glass bottles stuck their radiant necks out
of the sand, varieties of seaweed lay wasted like old mop
cloths, and the sea breeze was forever at work scrubbing
sand on everything that interrupted its movement. And
then, the crows—everywhere. The sea was full of them.
We watched them as they scampered, all at the same
instant, lunging and snatching after a piece of bread or any
desirable or shiny object—they made one-legged, lop-sided
landings, flipping and flailing in the sea breeze and colliding
into each other without caring a damn about anything.
And then after eating the piece of bread or whatever they
scavenged, they played among themselves with the wild
abandon of children still learning the rules of the game. In
some sense, the crows embodied the spirit of the city itself.
To me, they looked like litter with wings.

A couple had veered too close to us. The boy was
wearing tight jeans and in one of his hands he was turning
a keychain. They had their backs toward us and were
walking toward the sea with their bodies rubbing each
other's. The boy put his arm around her. He snuggled his
face in the girl's hair and kissed her on the neck.

'Haha! Did you see that?' I exclaimed to Sadeq.

I realized he had been looking at them for some time.

'Yes,' he said, not taking his eyes away from them.

'Just look at the guy! He's got the face of a shaved
chicken. Even *he's* got a girl.'

They took off their sandals where the wet sands began
and then began walking barefoot toward the water. At one

point, the girl stopped and pulled the boy back with his sleeve. She pointed him toward the footprint he'd just made on the sand. The boy bent down to look at the footprint closely and clutched the girl's bare ankle. Both of them laughed as she tried to release her leg from his grip.

'You don't need a face to get a girl, my dear,' Sadeq said, still holding his stare. 'You need balls that weigh two grams more than the rest of them. That's all.'

~

I am sitting with Baba on the roof of a tall building and we are both looking down. It is like flying, really—so little noise, full of air and happiness. You look below and think the world is a lovely thing playing many games. Cars are small, buildings have shapes, and everything moves in regular clumps within the straight lines of the roads.

'You see, my son, a city is all about how you look at it,' he says looking at me. 'We must learn to see it in many ways, so that when one of the ways of looking hurts us, we can take refuge in another way of looking. You must always love the city.'

I sit with him and imagine myself going up even higher, on some even taller building, as high as the sky itself. I imagine everything becoming so small that the world becomes a dot. A dot full of games. I see that little dot in my head and feel elated because it has all the cars, roads, buildings, Baba, I and Amma and my school. Everything.

That is how I first desire the city.

'So should we go and eat something? Do you see a bun-kebab stall here?' he said flicking the last chickpea in his mouth. But it missed its mark as he abruptly turned around. Two policemen stood behind us, open collars; the one with the baton had tapped Sadeq's shoulder.

'What are you two doing here oye?' one of them, who looked like the senior officer, asked.

'Nothing. Talking. What's wrong?' Sadeq replied.

'Talking? Ha!' he turned to the other and winked. 'We know what *that* means. What are you two *really* doing?'

'O why don't you speak, oye?' he paused to examine us, and then his belligerent tone turned malicious. 'Have we caught you doing something, eh?'

I felt my tongue disappear.

'What do you mean, sir?' Sadeq replied, his face flushed.

'What do I mean? Hmm.' His baton began tracing Sadeq's arm. It jumped to his waist and curved around his pelvis and hovered there for a few seconds and then started touching up his testicles. Sadeq twitched.

'Skipping school to have some one-to-one fun, eh?' he sneered. 'Let's take them to the station. We can teach them about some *real* one-to-one fun there,' he indicated to the other fellow.

'Sir, sir, we are just students, sir,' I blurted. 'We are not skipping school, sir. It's the last day of our exams and we got off early and thought we should come here...'

He wasn't listening. He asked for our IDs and told the other policeman, who was the junior officer, to take down our names and school names. Then he walked ahead and we followed behind him with the junior officer. After we had walked a little, the senior policeman stopped outside a paan stall to get a pack of cigarettes. When he was gone, Sadeq said to the junior guy who was standing with us, 'Can something be done? You know with some fees we can pay here?'

The second fellow looked at us sympathetically, 'Hmmm... I can try. Do you have something?'

'Yes, yes,' I said, and started pulling out the money from my pocket. Seeing the one-rupee bills, he was irritated and said, 'Are you kids messing with me? See the sir's shoulder—he has *two* stars!' He turned to Sadeq, 'What do you have?'

Sadeq turned his pockets and took out one ten-rupee note. He grabbed it. 'Okay, go. I will speak to Sir. No no keep those,' he pointed to my handful of one-rupee notes I was pushing toward him.

Both of us walked in the other direction as fast as we could, almost running. It was strange, because we were next to the open sea, always in sight, no place to hide, and they were right behind us. For all I knew, they could arrest us again for running away while in custody.

'Should we throw a rock at him? Smash the bastard's head?' Sadeq said in a vengeful tone.

'What? At who?'

'It's easy, they won't be able to catch us. Look at the bellies of those fuckers. They won't come after us. We can just run away. What do you say?'

'No!' I said incredulously.

'It's easy. We'll just hit them and get out, get on a bus or something.'

'No! It will get us into trouble! You don't fight with crazy men on the streets.'

'But the bastards... they...' his hardened face suddenly broke into tears. I stood there watching him as he tried to push his tears back into his tough exterior.

I did not know what to do. He covered his face with his elbow and sobbed. Finally, I put my arm around him. 'Let's sit.' I glanced back; the policemen were walking away from us in the other direction.

Sadeq sat with me on the ledge, sniffling, rubbing his eyes. I felt calm myself. The air was punctuated with his sniffles. We did not speak.

I was looking toward the sea: the waves arriving calmly then scattering on the shore. One reared its head above the body of the water far away, gained shape nearing the shore and along its path, gulped many tiny wavelets, and then it hit the shore and simply dissipated and shimmered back into the sea.

Amazingly, I was not thinking of Sadeq or the policeman.
I thought of the old man. He seemed a man who existed
only in stories. I began remembering things he'd said that I
thought I had ignored. He said some really strange things.
'The only thing you have is what's inside of you. Be hungry
for your heart. Find it. Run away with it. Marry it. People
just forget their hearts and do philosophies. Huee huee!
When I run away I begin to *feel* my heart. I am usually in
that café, eating fruitcake—but don't tell anybody—it's
our secret, okay? Huee huee huee! And no, you can never
run away from fruitcake and chai. Huee hueeee!'

I realized the old man had given a voice to something
in me that had been buried under a different voice that
had imperiously ruled my life. I imagined sitting with this
old man in the café, listening to his stories, surrounded by
the shouting bus drivers and paan-sellers, and the hotel
waiters. I imagined shaking his hand again, travelling on
a bus with him. And even though I was only a reluctant
truant, I had no doubt that we were friends. The thought
made me happy.

Sadeq and I finally got on the bus to return. He had
gone completely quiet, and I did not wish to speak to
him anyway.

I wanted to stop at the Cantt Station and look for the
café but the bus conductor said no bus was going there and

instead would go straight to Shahrah-e Faisal from Teen Talwar. It was closed for some official function. 'Where do you want to go? Take out the money.'

I paid him the fare and looked at the sea in my window that we were rapidly passing by. I dreamed of being surrounded by it. I wanted to lose all land. I wanted to suspend myself in the vast blue, where the same sea re-enacts itself all around me. It was another way to look at the city. That was how I desired the city the second time.

SADEQ

Turning to Stones

ASMA AAPA'S STORIES HAD become strange. She did not tell me old stories any more. Stories like the ones about the clever cobbler who enters the king's palace by saying he's a rich merchant and is then helped by the princess who falls in love with him and makes him rich. Or that other story about the beggar who makes the king realize his mistake and the king rewards him by making him his vizier…Now her stories ended with strange problems like sadnesses that couldn't be cured. Not even with happy things.

'So,' Aapa said, smiling, rubbing cream on her hand. 'I have a new story for you. Have you brushed your teeth?' She asked, untying her black hair, brown in the lamplight. 'Take off your socks. No stories if you don't do as I say.' She turned out the lights in the kitchen and was checking the locks of the main door.

Aapa had said the blanket does not have heat of his own. So I was already in the blanket rubbing my hands and giving some heat to him. She came and sat on the bed.

And then she told me the story of a king whose body was turned into stone by his wife.

'The king, of course, did not know he was marrying a sorceress. He thought her a very, very beautiful woman. His viziers and counsellors cautioned him about marrying a woman he did not know, but he ignored them and followed his heart's desire and married this beautiful girl who had come to his court and won his heart. Some months after the marriage, they had a fight and she got angry and turned him—from his belly down—into stone.'

As she said this, her warm hand petted my belly under the blanket and I wondered if the king's stone body could feel warm hands.

'And then she took over his kingdom.' She paused. I waited for her to tell me how he got his old body back but she didn't say anything. So I asked.

'But didn't his friends and viziers look for him?'

'They did, but the sorceress-queen did not allow anyone to visit him in person. In fact, she made it known that the king had died. She even arranged a dummy funeral for him, and cried so much that everyone believed her. She locked him in her chamber where she visited him every night.'

'What's a chamber, Aapa?'

'A chamber, my dear, is a big, big bedroom, with a king-sized bed and lots of red velvet cushions. But,' she paused, 'here's the interesting part: the queen-sorceress returned to her chamber every night where the king was writing poetry, lamenting his condition and fate. She sat with him, and tenderly said words of love to him and asked him to read his poetry to her. She cried when he read. She then took his poetry and sang it on her one-stringed guitar, which she played to perfection. In those moments, there was no enmity, no hate, no bitterness between them, and the king would feel like he had done absolutely the right thing by marrying her. He forgot his pain and his stone body and all his animosity for this woman. When the queen's song was over he looked at her, thinking she would cure his body again. But she left him without saying anything. This happened every night till the poor king died.'

I was very sleepy. Aapa turned off the lamp. It would not be possible for a stone person to turn in his sleep, I imagined.

'So what did the poor king do if he wanted to take a bath?' I asked Aapa with my eyes closed.

She laughed a little. 'Well, the queen would bring him soap and a bucket full of water...'

In my head, I saw the crying king washing his legs of stone with sponge and soapy water, and foam and water sliding down his legs into a blue bucket...With his other hand, he was writing poetry on a piece of paper. His tears were slipping into the exact same curve on his face one after the other.

Aapa and I had come to spend our winter holidays with Nani in her apartment because Amma and Baba were out of our city, Karachi, and we were her grandchildren and we loved her. This was also the reason why Aapa washed Nani's dishes and her dirty clothes.

Nani's apartment building did not have any elevators so Nani couldn't go anywhere because she once dropped a full bottle of strawberry jam on her foot and fractured it. I mean nothing happened to the jam bottle, but she was crying when she called Amma. Yes, crying even though she's so old. But it was not at all like when I cry; because when I cry, I just cry and forget about everything else. I can tell you she cried because I saw a tear stuck in the corner of her eye when I went to see her in the hospital; she was sitting on the hospital bed behind a curtain with one foot swollen and raised on two or three or four pillows. She asked me to come close and then she kissed my head.

After this incident, whenever Nani left her apartment, two people had to lift her chair and bring her down (or up) the stairs. She would just sit on her chair and talk to the men who were carrying her.

There were other things wrong with her too. She had a cut on her elbow which released a strange yellow substance and dirtied her clothes and made her irritated. She bandaged her elbow with her one hand and did it even better than the doctor who did it with two hands. The doctor said this himself.

Nani, Aapa and I had our breakfasts, lunches and dinners together. Nani was always asking Aapa if she liked some boy in the family and when she would get married.

'My girl, I tell you. You have already studied more than all the girls in our family and extended family. There is no point in studying further. See, listen to me now. You have to get married eventually, right?'

'Yes, Nani. But not now. I have to study,' Aapa said.

'Why do you have to waste your time in studying? All the rest of the girls are doing it, why are you acting so special? The time you are with me you should spend in learning how to take care of the house. I will teach you how. You should start taking care of this house. You will learn...'

During most other times, Nani was usually talking on the phone in her room—about getting people married in the family, who was ready, who suited who. She would also be asking people to come and see her. But no one visited her.

~

Every night, before we went to bed and Aapa told me stories, we spent time with Nani. We put her to sleep before we slept ourselves. It is good to take care of people.

Nani sat on the bed with her hair spread on her shoulders, all red and white and wet, like a mess, dripping water on her neck and clothes (her hair was red because they were white and she put henna in it; it even smelt like henna—cool and dirty). I saw her usually with her hair tied in a long red-and-white braid, but when she let it down, her face looked strange and I was a little afraid to go near her.

Nani's room was clean and smelt of a special musk she got from a special perfumer. She liked the colour white. So everything in the room was white, except for the wooden furniture. Even her books with yellow pages had white covers and the carpet had white sheets on it.

'I will not clean anyone's hair in my room. Pick that up. There...' she said pointing to a certain part of the sheet. 'If you have a problem of hair falling, put this special oil, but clean your hair from my room. I should not see anyone's hair on my sheets. I don't have servants in this house.'

Sitting on her bed she surveyed the room for broken hair or specks of dust. To avoid any dust in the room, she kept the windows closed. And everyone was required to check their feet for cleanliness before stepping into her room. The kitchen was in between the three rooms of her apartment. She said she washed and cleaned it three times every day. Now Aapa washed and cleaned it twice every day. Only once throughout the day she opened the windows, and that was before she went to sleep. She liked to get some fresh air before going to bed.

That night Aapa was massaging Nani's shoulders and I was pressing her aching feet. After this, Aapa had to oil her hair, prepare a list of the daily expenses and then line up Nani's medicine.

'Come my dear. Come here. Press my legs.' I sat on the floor and she sat on the bed. (Her legs were too fat for my hands.) After pressing her legs for some time, I was bored so I stopped and stared at the moth sitting on the tube light. It was not moving. I wondered what it was thinking (but how much could it think anyway with that small tiny head).

I started looking out of her window from which I saw a boy in a shalwar and sleeveless undershirt biting his fingernails and rummaging through clothes piled on a bed. Suddenly I felt Nani's leg shake. 'Umm Hmmm...' She glared, raising the eyebrows of her little eyes. 'You should never look in other people's houses. Understand?' I resumed pressing her legs. After a while, I looked again and I noticed the boy looking through our window; his eyes were following Aapa as she moved in the room.

~

Aapa started leaving the house in the afternoons. This was during the time Nani was taking the after-lunch nap. Aapa washed the dishes quickly and then let the water gush down on the already-washed dishes. She told me to wear a pair of big blue rubbery slippers and not to close the water tap. She told me to play or do-whatever-you-want wearing the rubbery slippers that were too big for my feet. They slapped wetly on the kitchen floor. (I liked the slapping sound they made—it was like bursting a nice plastic bag full of air.) The first time she left, she brought her face close to mine and her long wet hair fell forward and covered her face on the sides. I felt I was entering a dark place with the shampoo-smell of her hair. 'I am just going out for a little bit to see the girl who lives one floor up. I will come before Nani wakes up. If something happens, come and get me from her apartment. But do not take off those slippers, understand? I will bring you something when I go shopping.' And then she left hurriedly.

When she's in the kitchen, I play and talk to her as she is working. But now no one was there. I felt alone with the water gushing, the big slippers slapping and the feeling that Nani was breathing in her sleep in the other room.

The kitchen floor was grey and divided into big squares; each square had many little stones of many colours just spread about. It was like someone had dropped all those stones—white, dirty white, brown, red-brown, dark grey— and then just rolled them into the floor with the cement and made squares around it.

I thought about what each stone was saying to the other stone. They were talking about changing places. One of them wanted to turn and push the other guy away, while the other one wanted to leap into the other square, which had less stones. He thought it was like jumping into the sea, which had high waves and bobbing heads.

Aapa returned quietly. I noticed she had left the door slightly open. Her white face was a little pink and she was smiling. She did not speak with me and went quickly to our room and closed the door.

~

'But Aapa, if the king was a very intelligent king, as you said, why did he marry that evil sorceress, Aapa?' I asked when we were sitting on the bed and she told me her head ached, so no stories tonight.

'Well, the problem was he did not ask himself why he was marrying her,' she said.

'Hain? You mean he married her without asking and all that? But his viziers asked him, no?'

'Yes, but when his old vizier tried to ask such questions, the king got angry and threatened to get the old man lashed to death.'

'But why didn't he ask such questions?'

'Because he was asking himself different kinds of questions,' she said without looking at me.

'What are different kinds of questions?'

'I don't know. Don't ask me. I have a headache.'

I don't know why she was angry. But she was angry. So I turned my head and started looking at the lamp. There was an ant walking on the lampshade. It seemed like a dot of darkness walking on the floor of light.

'I am turning off the lamp,' she said.

'No,' I said. Because I wasn't sleepy and I was watching the ant.

I felt her hand taking my hand and then she kissed my neck. And then she put her face on my pillow.

'When the king turned to stone, he used to think about that moment when his vizier asked him questions about that girl. The king would curse that moment and himself for taking such a rash decision. But then he realized that he could not have asked himself about the girl, because he was in love with her...'

I turned on the pillow and looked at her.

'It is like this,' she said. 'The king was a different person when he was in love. Now that he was turned to stone, he was a different person.'

'But I did not ask that. I asked why didn't he ask questions about that evil woman?'

'My dear, you are not one person. You have many people in you, and each one can ask only some kinds of questions.'

I did not know what this meant. So I just kept on looking at her. She smiled, 'Go to sleep. I will tell you another story tomorrow.'

~

So that I wouldn't get bored in the afternoons when she left, Aapa bought me three little chicks—pink, yellow and red—from the man who comes on the cycle every day outside Nani's building and sells little chicks. Nani was angry and said these chicks would come into her room and dirty the whole place and she couldn't clean bird shit at this age in her life. But Aapa and I promised her that we would close all the doors when I played with them in the kitchen so that they could not go into any rooms.

I named them: the pink one was Ta, the yellow one was Za, and the red one was Kha. I wanted a box to make their home, because the man on the cycle said they must have a home. Nani gave me a big-sized oil can. But when I put the chicks in it they couldn't stand and slipped on the oil stuck to the bottom of the can. So I got a little carton for them. I made three windows in it so that they could look out into our house when they were bored. There was no door because I did not want them to go out whenever they wanted. They had to ask me and then I would take them out and put them wherever I wanted. I played with them in the kitchen when Nani was sleeping and Aapa was out and all the doors were closed. They were good children.

So Aapa was out that day and I wore my big slippers and took them out and told them to stand straight and listen to me. But the pink one, Ta, would not look at me. I was telling him that he should listen to me otherwise I would punish him by putting him in the slippery oil can, where he would just slip and slip and get tired and would not be able to play with the rest of us. But then suddenly he ran after a line of little ants. I was wearing my slippers and I ran after him and by mistake, I did not realize, I stepped on Za. Quickly I picked him up. He was hurt. I think it was the slipper that had hurt him. He was blinking one of his eyes very, very slowly. I ran out to look for Aapa.

I was quickly climbing up the stairs in those big slippers, which was difficult, and they were making so much noise. I reached one floor up and there were two doors there and I did not know which one Aapa was behind. Then I heard footsteps and I saw her coming down the steps from one more floor up. Her face was very red and she looked at me with anger.

'What is it? Why are you coming here?'

I lifted Za in my hand to her, 'He is dying.'

It looked like she did not even hear me. She said, 'Wait.' And then she ran back up the stairs. She came back and took Za and looked at him. She was panting a little. 'Hmm, it is dead, I think. What happened?'

'Can't we take him to the doctor?' I asked.

She did not say anything. She just smiled when I said this.

When we came down, the door was locked. We knocked and Nani opened the door. She stood in front and asked us where we went without asking her.

Aapa replied quickly, 'His chick had run out. We left in a hurry to get it.'

Nani looked at her. 'But you were upstairs, weren't you? Did it run up the stairs?'

Because I had started to cry (a little), Aapa did not reply to her and tried to stop me from crying. She caught Ta and Kha and put them in their box.

The tap was turned off. I passed by Nani, slapping the

big slippers on the floor. We knew she was angry. That night, we buried Za in a flower pot that had only mud in it and said special prayers for him.

~

Nani worked with Aapa in the morning. She made Aapa do all the work. Aapa made breakfast; then she cleaned the house and then made lunch. Nani was mostly on the phone in the mornings. Then she would have her lunch and the nap. She woke up and then we all had tea and biscuits and other things like nimko and then she went and talked on the phone till dinner.

Aapa and Nani spoke very little. And that night after Za died, Nani did not speak to Aapa during dinner and not even afterwards when we were in her room before going to bed.

Nani was speaking with me a lot. She asked me if I could read. She gave me a book of hers (yellow pages, white cover), pointing out the page she wished me to read. I tried to read, but I was reading very slowly and making a lot of mistakes. She corrected me as Aapa oiled her hair.

When Aapa said, 'Come on, let's go. Time to sleep.' Nani said, 'He will sleep with me tonight.'

So I looked at Aapa when she said, 'Good night,' and smiled.

It was dark in the room and I was facing the other way on the bed. Nani said, 'So what do you do in the afternoons?' She took my hand in her hand. Her hand was a little nicely cold because she washed her hands before sleeping.

'I play with Ta, Za and Kha. Otherwise I just play with something else.'

'Where's Aapa?'

'She's working in the kitchen.'

'Does she go out?'

I was quiet. I was afraid to tell her that Aapa goes out to meet the girl who lives one floor up. So I just acted like I was sleeping.

Nani asked again, 'Are you asleep already? What was she doing today? Why were you wearing her slippers?'

'What? I don't know, Nani jaan. I am feeling sleepy.'

'Hmm.' She did not say anything then. She kissed my head and said, 'Sleep now. Tomorrow I will cook something special for you. You like halwa?'

I found it difficult to sleep with Nani because she was snoring loudly and she held my hand in hers. After some time, I pulled my hand away and got off the bed.

'Where are you going?' she asked in her sleep.

'To the other room,' I said.

'Watch your step,' she said.

Aapa was awake. She opened the door when I knocked on it. When I told her that Nani asked about her afternoon visits, her eyes grew big and she covered her face and said, 'What did you tell her?'

'I said I don't know.'

She became quiet and said, 'Go to sleep.'
I could not see her face because it was very dark.

~

After that Aapa stopped going out in the afternoons and Nani sometimes came to check what we were doing. She asked Aapa about things she had given her to do and checked how she did them. But Aapa did not look happy and she became quiet as well. She would not even talk to me while she was washing dishes and cleaning the kitchen.

I saw Nani watching and standing near the chicks' home a few times. She asked me about them and I told her what they did and what they talked to each other about all the time. I also told her they missed Za very much because he was the nicest one of them all.

Kha (the red one) also died. I don't know why. I think because he ate dirty ants and dust. Even though I told him so many times to only eat what I gave him (I gave him bread crumbs and rice and other clean and nice things) and not to go around eating everything he found on the ground, but he ate all those dirty things and one day when I woke up I saw he was limping and could not stand. He did not eat or start running when I took him out of his house. He just sat there with his eyes closed.

I was sad when he died. And for two or three or four nights, Aapa did not tell me any new story as well. 'I don't know any stories about chicks.' She also said she did not know any more stories. One or two times she read them from the magazines. They were happy stories but I did not like them. She could not even tell me why the evil sorcerer did not marry the princess and why he was waiting for the prince to arrive, wasting so much time. Aapa did not like that story either. She seemed angry.

Only Ta was left to play with me. In the afternoon, Aapa quietly took out the phone from Nani's room for a few minutes and took it inside her own room. (It had a long wire, not like the phone in our house, which cannot be taken anywhere because it has such a short wire.) I played with Ta when Aapa was talking quietly on the phone but Ta did not like to play with me. He liked to be alone. He ate what I gave him and sometimes jumped as well, but he did not run like Za and Kha. So I sat in the corner and watched him walk around the kitchen.

~

Then one night Aapa said she would tell me a new story. 'The Speaking Bird and the Singing Tree'.

Once upon a time there was a beautiful girl who was always sad for no reason. She had three princes who loved her and wanted to marry her. She liked one of them but she could not express her love to him, because if she declared her love for him the other two might kill him. So one day, that sad girl was sitting outside her house waiting for the vegetable hawker to buy vegetables when this very, very old woman suddenly appeared and said, 'My lovely girl, the reason you are unhappy is because you don't have the speaking bird and the singing tree.' The girl was surprised when she heard this. She asked immediately, 'Where can I find them, my dear old woman?'

The old woman told her where she should go to find them. They were in the Dark Mountains (they were Dark Mountains because all their rocks were dark grey). But the old lady warned her, 'Remember: when you are climbing the mountain, don't turn around and look what's behind you. Remember that, just don't turn around.'

The girl agreed to go. But when she told her plans to the princes who loved her, they persuaded her not to go and said they would go instead and get the speaking bird and a branch of the singing tree for her. In return, she promised to marry whoever brought her the singing tree and the speaking bird.

Because she loved one of the princes and wanted him to win, she only told him about the warning of the old woman. 'Remember, don't turn when you are climbing the mountain,' she whispered in his ear as she saw him off.

The first prince climbed in haste and his foot slipped and to save himself from falling, he looked back and immediately turned to stone. The second prince when climbing thought that someone was throwing stones at him. He turned to see who it was and as soon as he turned, he turned to stone. The third prince, the one the girl loved and wanted to marry, was also the most cautious and intelligent of the three. When he was climbing the mountain, he saw many sculptures of young men. He paused to examine them. Suddenly he heard some noise. He remembered the warning so he did not turn and continued his journey onward. As he went further, he started hearing even stranger noises—like witches coming after him. But still he did not turn. Finally, everything became calm and peaceful. He was very tired and thought he had reached the end of his journey. His heart was full of joy. He looked up to the sky full of stars and felt the cool breeze. He wanted to talk to someone about it. Suddenly, he heard the voice of the beautiful girl he loved. As soon as he turned to look, he, too, turned to stone.

'The rest of the story I will tell you tomorrow,' Aapa said. I said all right. I knew what was going to happen anyway. The girl would go to the Dark Mountain herself and get the bird and singing tree. But what would happen to the princes who had turned to stone?

~

The next afternoon Aapa and Nani had to go visit the neighbours for Qur'an khwani. So in the afternoon, Nani and Aapa wore nice clothes and went next door where lots of women with colourful clothes were also coming and taking off their slippers outside the house.

After a while, I got very bored. Ta was not playing. He just went and stood in a corner, and I missed Za and Kha. I took him into the balcony, which he liked. I had to stop him always from going near the edge where he could fall off. I wanted to show him something in the big ground in front of us, but instead we talked about the moon. I told Ta that the moon is not supposed to be there in the morning because it is the sun's time but Ta had gone back inside the house. I put him in his house again and went out to look for Aapa.

I could not find her slippers in all the slippers lying outside the door of our neighbour where the Qur'an khwani was happening. Then I climbed the stairs and smelt the perfume she put on herself in the afternoons. I ran up the stairs, two flights, and there I saw Aapa and the boy who had been looking into our house from his window without a shirt. He was wearing a shirt now and had his hand behind Aapa's back and his mouth was on her neck. I shouted, 'Oye! What are you doing?'

Aapa pushed him away and came toward me. 'Why, why have you come here?' When she came near me, she stopped and covered her face with her hand. I turned and I saw what Aapa saw: Nani was standing halfway up the stairs looking at Aapa and the boy.

What happened after that was just noise and shouting. Nani started shouting and all the women from the Qur'an khwani came out. And then Nani started crying, saying that oh our honour is destroyed our honour is destroyed. This girl has destroyed our honour. All we had was our honour and this girl destroyed it all.

Someone told me to go inside, you are a child, and then locked me in from outside.

I stood near the door and heard lots of cries and shouts. When Aapa came back with Nani both of them were crying and Nani was angry and shouting at her. Aapa's hair was over her face. She went straight into the room and closed the door and locked the door. Nani was cooking food and kept on saying I told your parents I told them that they should get this girl married. The world is already so corrupt. I told them. Now see what has happened. Our honour is lost. Now who is going to marry this girl? The whole world knows. This girl has destroyed our honour. We're faceless. We can't show our face to anyone. It is all gone, our honour, our respect, all gone...

When Nani went into her room that night, I took some water for Aapa and knocked at her door. She opened after a long time. She was crying.

~

After that Aapa did not speak with anyone for a long time and just cried. Nani also kept on saying things to her as if she was saying them to herself but really she was saying them to Aapa.

I really wanted Aapa to finish that story of the singing tree and speaking bird.

We went back to our house when Amma and Baba returned. Nani told them what Aapa had done. She made it look so bad. Baba was very angry and Amma started crying. But then we went home and things became all right but Aapa was not allowed to go out of the house without permission. And Baba stopped talking with her properly.

The end of the story was this. Aapa told it to me one night in our home a long time afterward.

The girl waited for the princes to come back for a long time but when they did not return she set out to get the speaking bird and singing tree herself. When she was scaling the Dark Mountain she saw the prince she loved as a stone sculpture. She also heard all kinds of sounds and screams but she didn't turn and reached the top of the mountain. There she found the speaking bird, which greeted her and told her where she could find the singing tree. The girl went to the singing tree and broke a branch for herself. The girl then tapped the branch on all the people who had turned to stone and they became human again. They thanked the girl and went home.

'So, does she marry the prince she loved?' I asked.

'I don't think so.' Aapa said. She got off the bed and straightened the blanket over my feet. 'When she tapped the branch of the speaking tree on them and they all turned into humans again, they were all the same to her. The one she loved and those she didn't had turned all the same.'

I thought about that but I did not understand it so I asked her if she knew any more happy stories. She said, 'Yes, I do. It's a very short story though.'

She told me this story about a little prince who kept crying because he wanted the moon. He wanted to play with it like a toy. Each night he would look at the moon and start crying. Then suddenly his mother, the Queen, thought of an idea. She brought out a large bowl of water in which the moon was reflected. When the little prince saw the moon in the water, he started playing with it.

After that story I gave Ta a little tub of water so that he could look at himself and not miss Kha and Za. But when I came back to play with him, I saw he had drowned in it. His beak was open and he was just lying there dead and his pink feathers were filled with water.

I buried him like that, soggy and cold, with Za and Kha in the flower pot. I also understood why Aapa stopped telling me happy stories.

Good Days

IT'S ONE THING WHEN you're cruising on a steady honk, going *wham wham* past everything, and one thing else when you go slow and easy, reading number plates, matching them with a number inside your head.

'2219, na?' Pannoo shouts. '2219! I found it!' His hand flies off the steering wheel and flaps in the air.

Chuchu's on the passenger seat. He leans into Pannoo's side of the windscreen. 'Where?' he asks.

'Ha! That's 22-7-9!' I say, laughing. 'You so chutiya, Pannoo!'

Pannoo realizes he's misread. Chuchu sees it too. For two seconds it's like their brains are parked in darkness.

'Ugh,' Chuchu grunts.

'Can't you READ?' I laugh louder. 'Oye Pannoo, you smoked UP? Chuchu, you should get somebody who can READ.' I feel a surge of happiness for saying this to Pannoo, to his face, to his fucking chicken chutiya face I love to loathe.

It gets him all right. He turns around and I see my face—a blue twisted oval—in his big bad shades.

'What happened, mister chut?' I smile. 'Are you trying to scare me? Hoohoohoo, I'm scared.'

He keeps looking at me—for three seconds straight. The car is moving at a good thirty or forty or something. It's scary. This chutiya is capable of all things. And like that: ALL things. Days back, he bit off somebody's earlobe in a friendly scuffle and then spit the piece of the guy's ear into his palm. I don't want him to keep looking at my face, so I point to the windscreen and shout, 'Watch it!' And that does it—he hits the brakes without even turning around. The car screech-stops in the middle of the road and for half a second we are eating the air from the shock. Then we are banged in by something. My face hits the seat and I get a rash knock in my jawbone.

I turn around and see the traffic curving around our car. But there's nothing behind us.

'Nothing happened, right?' I ask.

Pannoo's hands are clamped on the steering wheel. 'Shut him up, Chuchu,' he says. Clearly, he doesn't care what we've hit.

'Shut up you both—' says little Chuchu, acting like our big brother. He gets out of the car; I follow.

We find a motorcycle half-buried beneath the rear of our car. Chuchu's helping a middle-aged man stand up. The man's short and fat and looks like a tree stump; clumps of hair climbing out of his open shirt collar, and a lush beard cropped close to his face. It's a *nice* beard, actually; I'd like to have one like it one day. I pull out the motorcycle from under the car and walk it to him on the footpath. It's all scratched up from the side.

I pat the man on his shoulder in a friendly way, 'Just watch how you drive, boss.'

'Did I say anything to you, HAAN!' he starts yelling. 'Did I say it was YOUR mistake!' He's angry at us for something else I feel. Some anger already inside him boils its way into his voice. He looks funny, like a fuming truck. I look at him for two seconds and then I start laughing. He twists his mouth a little and stares at me.

'You have a nice beard,' I say, laughing.

That's when people start gathering. What happened? What happened?

We return to the car, leaving the guy holding his arm.

I am still laughing.

'What? Any trouble?' Pannoo asks.

No answer.

'Why is he laughing? What's so funny?' Pannoo asks again.

'Nothing. The man's hurt his arm,' replies Chuchu.

'What was he saying? Did he ask for money?'

Chuchu doesn't reply.

'Are you going to tell me—what was the man SAYING?' Pannoo asks again.

'He was saying NOTHING!' Chuchu bursts out. 'Let's find the fucking car, shall we?'

He gets like this, Chuchu; hurts and smarts like a fucking human being. Still too soft for our kind of work.

~

The plan is simple: to make it impossible to locate 2219. That's my ticket to watch Chief getting kicked in the balls and, who knows, to put an end to this company.

This company has a name: Chief Security Services, but when Chief and I started out, we simply used to call it Uchakkas—very loosely, *The Lifters*. Our task is to locate and recover cars that are on the List.

The List comes from the bank; of cars whose installments have not come in for three months or more. We have the bank's licence and court's permit to do this, but at the end of the day, it's a private business. That is, nobody's going to step in and save us if somebody sends a bamboo ripping up through our ass and beyond. Get this: nobody. The good thing is we have guns and can shoot in self-defence. We have court protection for that.

How I joined this business is a story. I was out of college and doing nothing when Chief asked me to become a partner in his company. That was two years back. It would be just the two of us, he said. We'll keep it low key; share the profits—forty, sixty.

Forty per cent looked good to me, especially because I was not doing any of the accounts or anything in the office. He explained how it worked. He got me a gun, the permits, and for transport we were going to ride his bike. We were set.

Our first case, we were looking for a maroon Nissan Sunny that had vanished; no traces. We tried the standard methods: called the guy up, said words to the women in the house, sent a few drunken boys to smash a few things outside his house, but the bastard knew somebody who knew somebody-lawyer who sent legal notice to the bank for harassment who sent bamboos up our chutes and we had to stop the indirect methods. Then one day early in the morning, too early, Chief called and said he had picked up the trail of the car.

When we got there we found the car outside the man's house; his wife was in the driver's seat, brushing her cheek with a blush-on when Chief walked up from the side and pulled out the gun at her. She howled and flashed her nail-polished hands at his face. He backed up a couple of steps and kicked the side of the door, and yelled at her out of his gut, his sticky early morning spit flying out of his mouth. When she stepped out of the car, Chief caught her arm and yanked her aside and got into the car. He was about to turn the ignition when a stinking meat-heap of a man walked out the door with a pistol hanging in his hand. He pointed it at Chief's car but before he could fire, I fired two shots in the air. He sneaked back in and fired at my bike. I didn't get hit but the fucker tried. We drove off to the police station to get the FIR registered and report the car as 'Recovered'. That was the first case, and it taught me my most important lesson: even when it gets messy, get out as cleanly as possible.

But I knew nothing about the insides of the business, did not know how much money we were making. I just kept what the Chief gave. But then I noticed him get rich: in three months he got a new bike and in nine months he got his new car. On my side, in nine months I had just enough to get comfortable on a new bike; sure, I had other expenses, but I could not afford a new car, no way. So I told Chief, it doesn't look to me to be adding up. He got angry without even asking what I meant and shot back saying that I was accusing him of stealing the money. I said I said no such thing but in all that shouting he let on that he had been keeping a percentage for the office and extra for his wages as an accountant and manager and other things. Then he started pulling out the account books and tried explaining everything. But by that point I just didn't care. I knew he was a cheat. Then I got loud and he lost it and then we fought properly without any holding back.

That same day I fought with Sehr.

Sehr was this girl I had lost my head for. I was blinded by her, but I did not know what I wanted from her except that I wanted her completely. She told me to quit this job and find something else. I tried to explain to her that this work, yes, it looked dirty, but it was totally legal. I even showed her the licence and court permits for everything. She did not agree. Came a point when she said she was going to marry somebody else. It was her age to get married and I wasn't looking like a good idea to her. I was in pieces. As I said, we had this conversation the same day I fought with Chief and for a month, I didn't go to work or wash my face; just kept trying to understand why this happened, why that happened. I still don't understand.

When I went back, Chief told me I was no longer required at the company—and I should at least wash my face before showing up for work. He told me firmly, 'You are a bloody nobody around here. The company owes you nothing. Go.'

He thought that I'd feel angry and insulted and quit the job, but I was hungry and tired thinking about Sehr and why she did what she did and who the fuck was she going to marry and why. I did not say anything to Chief. I turned around and apologized instead. He was surprised, so surprised that for three seconds he said nothing and looked at my face to see if I was being funny. Then he said, 'Fine. I don't hold grudges and don't want you to have any either. If you need work you can work for commission— like other boys. Just that you are no partner remember. And you can be fired like other boys.'

I knew other boys could be fired for No Reason.

That's how. That's how he insulted me. But I knew I was tired and hungry and so I kept quiet and asked him if he had 5000 rupees I could borrow for a couple of days. He gave me the money and shook my hand.

That day on, he kept things uneasy between us: kept me out of important cases, delayed my payments, and once even offered that I could take a little bonus for all my previous work—as a token of his love—and go find work somewhere else. It was tempting—all that free, extra money—but I told him, 'No, I am happy to work for commission just like the other boys. It gives me a job.'

I gave him no reason to be suspicious. My car recovery ratio was a shocking 100 per cent. And so one day, I was told I was being put on the Team for Special Cases.

Thing was Chief was in trouble. He had lost real money betting on the Pakistan cricket team in the Cup final. The guy he owed money to was a political party worker known for guns and steel. Two days back, the guy visited the shop and yelled at Chief that he was going to rip his ass up if he didn't pay up in three days. So now Chief had ideas.

Instead of returning the car to the bank, we had to bring it to the workshop, where after the necessary rebranding (change the number plate, new papers, all that), Chief was going to sell it for cash. It was not legal but it was smart: instead of turning the defaulted cars in to the bank, you sell them at half the price. The police would treat the car as stolen, the bank could claim its money from the insurance, and nobody was ever going to go looking for the car.

This was not recovery any more. It was stealing. But the commission for this work was five times. I agreed to it immediately. But not for the money—not really—but to make up for my missing forty per cent. And everything else.

∼

The car smells sweet and blurry. Pannoo takes a drag while studying the backside of the Honda Civic in front of us. His face is pretty fucked. He's Chief's right-hand man. He gets to oversee the Special Cases.

On my right, a driver's half-drowsy half-nasty eyes are looking at me. He's got a brick-brown face, a thick moustache creeping up his unshaven cheeks. I know what he's seeing-thinking, seeing-thinking with all the smoke inside our car—ah, all the sweetly wafting smoke—I *know* he sees-thinks us to be a bunch of smoked-up bastards. Bastards he's telling us, look. BASTARD he's calling me. BASTARD!

I stop my thoughts and look deep into his right eye and load my face like I want to spit into his eyes and say 'FUCK YOUR MOTHER YOU MOTHERFUCKINGINGINGG—' but that's when I see a large cooking pot wobbling down the footpath behind him, spraying hot steaming chickpeas from its lidless mouth. A boy, young, tenish, runs after the pot. He slaps it on the head and it falls on its mouth with a loud metallic gulp. The chickpeas spill out on the road. The boy squats and starts to sweep them all wet and muddy into his palms. His face is sticky and dusty with sweat. He looks like he'll break into tears.

I have SEEN this bugger—*fucker*—before! Haha, he does the tears pretty well. Cars slow down, people pause to look. Once enough people are around, he lifts up his kurta, and lets the blood-seeping, whip-stripes on his back show. He tells you that he works for a contractor, who is his father or his uncle, who whips him for fucking up. You'd think his father/uncle/contractor beats his skin white with a hot ladle for spilling the stuff on the road. Yes, you'd think of a hot-ladled father-contractor-uncle yelling at the kid—*You fucker! You motherfucker! Oyeyooooooou!* Tha. Tha. Haha.

If I could get out now—right NOW—if I *could*—I'd knock his face off his shoulders and bang it into the tarmac. Blood would pool around his head and roll into the road cracks, leave a dark patch when dry and turn into tar. Everything you leave on the road turns like that, first dark then tar—that's how a fresh yellow banana gets killed on the road: it vomits its pulp, then turns black, then dry black and then nothing. NOTH—

'Look carefully now. We must find the car today, this is the most probable route.'

'Keep in the centre lane, keep looking, this is the route,' Chuchu tells Pannoo, me, anybody.

The smoke rolls upward, unscrewing the tight spaces at its centre and blurring the off-white matt-leather seat in front of me. I feel the hit in my head. I start missing her and the dark. My hands miss her. I miss her wet and vicious in that dark landing, doors of empty apartments on both sides. She smelled of sweat and sadness and patches of muffled strawberry perfume. She kissed me with immense sadness. I miss her with all the memory in my muscles.

I close my eyes and recline my head against the seat. With my dick so hard, I just got to go to sleep I think.

~

I got my revenge with Sehr. I stalked her for weeks, showed up outside her college, phoned incessantly at her home number, called and yelled at her close friends for being the reason of our break-up and sprayed the walls with her address and phone numbers so that all the dicks hanging out of pants everywhere could go and bang at her door and make her feel like without me she was just a slut in hell. I just stamped and stamped her with my boot. Her parents had to get their home phone number changed and change the college she went to.

Haha. She was hot.

There is another girl now. Asma. My bedroom window opens onto her grandmother's bedroom. That's how we first said 'Hello'. That first look and I knew she was warm and salty and just right. So later when I found her going down the stairs, I tried to make eye contact but she ignored her way past me. Then another time I just stopped her and told my name and said I wanted to be friends. She smiled, said, 'Thank you,' and disappeared. Came one day in the afternoon when I ran into her. She was sitting alone on the apartment stairs, humming some old Bollywood song. I started talking to her and that was it. From that day, we met every day in the afternoons on the stairs. I am here to live with my grandmother for a few months, she said. Till her parents returned. They were away trying out another city for a few months to see how it suited them to move for good. That was her story, she said.

She was different from Sehr. She didn't have any anger inside her. She was happy. Happier than happy. Her dark brown curly hair smelled of fresh shampoo and she had stories—of her little kid brother, of her mother's trunk whose inside nobody has seen, of her grandmother's belief that you should not cut your nails at night, or drop them on bare floors, because that affects your health and wealth. I laughed when she told me this about her grandmother. I asked her if she believed such things. She looked at me with a quizzical face—she said, 'Aren't stories always true?' I said, I don't understand. So she told me this story of a sorceress who turns her husband, the mighty Emperor, into stone, and visits him every evening so that she could feed him with her hands and talk to him and hear him recite poetry to her. 'She did that out of love. Because when he was the Emperor he was High and Mighty and did not care about how she loved him. When he turned into an invalid she could take care of him. You see? She did that out of love. Love makes you want to possess people. It makes you destroy the other person.' I didn't understand what the hell she meant in that story but for half a second I felt whipped at the back of my neck with the steel part of a belt. (I once got that in a fight.) It got me thinking about Sehr, about what I did to her. Did I hurt her so that she could know how much I loved her?

Afternoons, Asma and I sat on the stairs and laughed in low voices, and hummed Bollywood songs. In the fuzzy darkness of the apartment landings, her skin glowed and her eyes were always thinking something up. Up close, she was warmer than I had thought from a distance, but strangely, I could never bring myself to touch her. I never understood why.

She touched me. But it was different. Why is your eye so red, she'd ask, placing her fingers below the eye; or, do you have fever, the back of her hand on my forehead, on the side of my neck. When she touched, it left me muddled with feelings that I had never felt. I kept welling up with feeling when she touched. I did not dare touch her back because I knew if I touched her, my touch would be different. It would break something—something was going to happen to her, but more importantly, to myself first.

It scared me that I could not touch her without damaging her.

But yesterday, we met on the landing. Her grandmother was in the neighbour's house. She told me it was her last day. Her parents were going to return and she will go away to another city. That we should do something. She looked at me intensely but I did not know what she meant. Then suddenly she pressed my face in her hands and then before I had finished drawing breath, her mouth was on mine. Her skin, her hair and warm smell and sadness.

I exploded. I put my hand around her waist and then gathered my fingers in the small of her back. All I could think of was Sehr, how hard I was to her—HARD. And how gently this girl touches me. I held her to the wall and was kissing her neck when her little brother shouted, 'Oye! Kya karta hai!' After that I only remember her grandmother's large melting eyes.

~

We're at a traffic signal. From Chuchu's face it looks like he's crushing something behind his eyes. He's handsome in a black shirt, collar stiff and alert, soaking up the sweat coursing down his temples. I turn around to find the chickpea boy. Too late. But somewhere behind us he's still filling up his palms with chickpeas, wet and muddy, which he'll reheat and resell hot and steaming. I bet he will. And you will eat. Haha.

The girl in the car next door is wearing a sea-green sleeveless kameez. She's looking ahead with her elbow out of the car. Her glowing neck is bare and white. I stare into it. Taut white glowing neck, I'd like to eat. She glances at me and pauses, half-smile. I know how we look to her, I *know*: our heads like fish floating in an aquarium. She must be thinking of something to herself. Something about the boy who could touch her, who was allowed to touch her up in all the places. The soft cusp in her arms, white and warm. And her neck, the most eatable curve you'll dig your teeth into...

That chutiya Pannoo still has the joint. 'Give it to me,' I rap the seat near his shoulder. 'And roll up the window. You are fucking up.' The window's already up, I know. I just want to be a bastard to him. I want him to say something to me, something that angers me enough to crack his head open.

The joint's gone in a suck. I'm still hungry. Things taste sweeter when you have some hunger left to linger. You feel it hunting your head for buried things; digging into the fractures of your brain with its sharpened nails. It makes your breath warm and greedy.

The signal's green now. The girl next door is thumping the horn with the meat of her palm. Cars spill forward. We get ahead of her but then—she turns—left. I feel my pit turn into stone—

'2219! I saw it!' I yell. 'To the left! Behind us!'

'Behind! Behind us! Quick!'

'We cannot turn now!'

'What!'

'Fuck! FUCK!'

Pannoo hits the brakes and the accelerating cars behind us screech into each other. I hear three quick blows; the Suzuki pick-up behind us takes the hits, but we feel it too.

'Pannoo! BHANCHAUD!' Chuchu shouts and pulls out his gun. He turns in his seat and sits on his knees. Some cars go past us but the road before us all of a sudden is empty. Pannoo hits the accelerator and we lurch into the hole in the traffic in front of us. We race in with a loud constant honk. The traffic ahead of us slows but Pannoo keeps pressing.

'Turn at the next left, LEFT,' Chuchu shouts. Pannoo thrusts the car in front of somebody making the turn. The guy brakes and then honks like a real mother of fuck. I turn around and look at him in the face. It is that brown-brick-faced driver. I raise my fingers to my lips and flash the gun at him. The honk stops. Then we turn and zoom. We're traffic.

~

There's no 2219. We are parked at a tea-khokha, in front of us is Jinnah Hospital. I am sitting on the footpath, swallowing my tea. It's dirty hot and its sweetness sears my chest. Pannoo is fixing the car (some knocking in the engine). Across the road, an old man is trapped inside a rickshaw. He's trying to stand up but his body shakes and his muscles seem all out of power. He's probably here for a hospital visit.

My mind still ducks when trying to think of Asma. Her grandmother yanked her down the stairs by her hair. I watched her squeal but I didn't move an inch. Stood watching as if I was the victim, and she some sort of criminal. Nobody paid me any attention. Her grandmother pulled her down and at that moment I knew I will never see her again. It starts a sinking inside me.

'Are you sure you saw 2219?' Pannoo asks me, placing the teacup back on the car radiator. 'Was it black? Honda Civic?'

'No.'

Pannoo stands with his mouth agape. He keeps staring at me, keeps staring at me, keeps staring. I don't look.

I think: she's probably still in the apartment. I understood her better when she touched me, sucked me breathless. She wanted to give me something. What we exchanged mouth-on-mouth was pain. For a moment, I understand what I did wrong with Sehr: I wanted to possess her. That's how I destroyed her. Like the sorceress destroyed her husband because she wanted to possess him.

The motherfucking old man is still stuck inside the rickshaw. Now I can't even see him. He's collapsed on the seat, probably. And the rickshaw driver, instead of helping him get out, is leaping over to my side of the road. He's aiming for a paan shop. Fuck him. I am done with tea.

I cross the road and look inside the rickshaw. The old man, all bone and teeth, is lying stiff in his seat. He sees me peeping in and moves his hand to cover his pocket. I tap him on the shoulder, 'Baba ji, hold it.' I lean closer and lift him up in my arms out of the rickshaw. He lets out a weak grunt, which turns into feeble oomph, oomphs.

I sense a cool liquid on my left arm and my nostrils are invaded with a sickening smell. Suddenly I know why he couldn't move—there was a rotting fucking wound on the side of his stomach. The old man is panicked, he's staring into my face, oomphing. His body stiffer in my arms and I'm standing there thinking, What the fuck do I do now? I am also aware that my clothes stink of churs.

I see a man speeding toward me. He's pushing a wheelchair. 'Aay! What are you doing with my father?'

'Who? Oh!' I look at him with a forgotten look. 'Oh. I was… just trying to help… get him out of the rickshaw.'

I place the old man on the wheelchair and watch his son drive him away. I still feel the cool trace of the old man's wound on my forearm. There's numbness in my feet. Holding this man's limp bones has filled me with a strange kind of sadness. It was similar to when Sehr said she did not love me. That she would never love me. That she was going to marry somebody else. I feel that kind of darkness overcoming me. I throw around my hands to keep it from creeping down on me. And then I suddenly see it: I see Asma was wrong. Yes, she was lying with those stories. She knew she was lying. That she loved me when she kissed me. She did not want to destroy me. Her story was wrong. Love is not destroying; it's touching like she did, touch not to tear and snatch but to give something you cannot give because after giving it you will have nothing and the other person will take it all and still feel it's nothing. And it kills you because it's everything you have.

I realize I was mad at Sehr for this. I was angry because

she took everything I had and then said it wasn't good—not good enough.

My head swims. I feel deep within myself and think: What am I doing? I have nothing to give to anybody. I think of Chief and Pannoo. This work. Hot smoke rises in my chest. I feel seething dense smoke rising up and up through my chest in my brain. I stand there feeling it and then it maxes out and breaks and wafts into invisible wisps. Then it's gone. And then, I breathe. I am done. I am done with this work. Chief and Pannoo can go fuck each other forever. I am decided. Fuck this. Fuck this. Fuck this work. This snatching from everybody. Let Chief live with this business. I will go away. I am free.

I breathe, and it feels like for the first time I have done it in years. It feels empty and amazing. It feels like having found something to give.

Just then, across the road, Chuchu springs up from the footpath. His tea flings out from his cup and smashes a curve on the tarmac. He runs to Pannoo and points him to something. I follow his finger and I see the metallic side of a black Civic cruise past us.

Next moment Pannoo is in the car and whirring the engine madly. I am stranded on the wrong side of the road. Chuchu waves to me but there's still traffic and I can't go anywhere. Chuchu gets in and the car races out. I watch their car go after the Civic, and then I see a hand emerge out of Pannoo's window. He's waving me goodbye. Goodbye, motherfucker. BYE. I am done. Yes.

Then I see the hand that Pannoo's stuck out. It's not a goodbye. It's his middle finger.

A shot of poison surges through my brain.

I am not done with this work. Not yet, I suddenly know. I hate these people more than I love anything.

~

I go after them in a rickshaw. I spot them just before the Cantt Station turn: the Civic roughly cornered and Chuchu's gun on the car window. Pannoo is sitting in the car for back-up.

I see Chuchu swing the door open and grab the man's collar to yank him out. The man holds on tightly to the steering wheel. Chuchu throws a raw slap on his face. 'Get out of the car! All of you!' he screams.

They shuffle out of the car, a family of four. Two little boys. They are wearing shoes with lights in the heels that blink red and blue like police cars. When I join Chuchu's side, the woman has broken into sobs. She says to Pannoo, 'Don't hit. Take whatever you want. Just don't hit anybody.' I signal to her with my finger on the lips and push the family to the side of the footpath to let Chuchu take control of the car.

'The car does not start!' Chuchu yells. 'Bring him here! The bastard has a security lock somewhere—'

I signal to the man. Chuchu's slap loosened the blood-tap in his nose; his moustache looks like a curdle of blood. His face looks scared and disgusting. He walks to the car and kneels before the open door and scrambles his hand under the driver's seat where Chuchu is sitting. 'Here's a little bump,' he tells Chuchu. 'You will feel it if you press it firmly.' We hear a click.

'Hold your hand,' Chuchu tells him, trying to locate the exact spot. 'Where?'

'Here.'

'Here?'

'No here.'

'Here?'

'No. This, here.'

'WHERE IS IT, YOU FUCKER?' Chuchu crashes a punch into his back.

'Chuchu!' I hold his hand.

'You fuck with us, I shoot you right here,' he starts to yell at him. 'You hear that?'

The man is trembling. He sniffles on the blood drying in his nose. 'I can tell you an easier way if you let me sit in the seat.'

Chuchu pushes his gun into his belly. The man steps back. He gets out of the car and points the man to get in.

He sits in the driver's seat and splays open his legs. 'Slide your hand in like this—' he shows us the exact place where the hand must slide in. 'Just slide in your fingers. It's right here. Easy.' He clicks the switch again for us.

137

'Get out.' Chuchu gets in. This time he finds it. I tell the man to join his family in the corner and give him the instructions: no need to alert the police, no need to get angry. This car was overdue.

I tell Chuchu I need to drive. I can't sit with Pannoo. He says, 'What the hell, I am not doing this again with you two around.'

He moves out to Pannoo's car.

I follow Pannoo, I know. Standard operating procedure. It's all over.

I click the security switch and start up behind Pannoo's car. My throat is still sticky with the sweet tea and I am thinking of Asma's lips. I feel my heart clamped as I begin to follow Pannoo's car. I will never be able to get out of what I do, I know. I will be here, doing this. I will be snatching; breaking things, people. I feel a sinking inside of me.

Pannoo blinks the left indicator. He turns, I speed up, but then I brake the car completely. I am in a dream. I am holding the old man's paper-stuffed body and he has his hands up, waving to me. He's trying to tell me. His voice is too low, but then I realize that I do not want to hear him speak because he reeks of wounds.

I wake up with an explosion. The air in front of me shatters like glass and something tears into my side of the door. My head hits something. Hard.

Something.

Seconds later, I see a car lying crashed on its head. It's

Pannoo's and Chuchu's. And although I did not see it, I have a clear memory of that car flipping in the air and a gush of heat blowing in from beneath it and engulfing me. It was fire and light and air and for once I saw clearly.

The World Doesn't End

My brother, an ambulance driver, was on duty on the day of the Cantt Station bomb blast. Now only God is witness to what he saw or heard, but when he returned from his duty later that night, his condition was beyond description. I was asleep, but my mother says he walked in the door without his soul in him. His collar was torn open and shirt buttons were all broken as if he had been in a fight.

At first, he seemed all right, a little quiet, as you are usually after facing such a horrendous atrocity. He even said, 'Yes, bring the dinner,' when she asked him if he was hungry. But then when he saw the food, he immediately left and locked himself up in the bathroom.

I must mention that my brother, aside from being very diligent and dutiful, was also a lively and spirited boy. He was nineteen years old.

My mother woke me up and told me that Akbar had locked himself inside his bathroom and was not replying to her. My mother and I stood outside the bathroom door trying to persuade him to come out, but he wasn't replying to anything we were saying. Then we heard vomiting, followed by little shrieks that turned into loud sniffles.

'Are you feeling all right, Akbar?' I asked. No reply. 'Akbar? Answer me.'

'Akbar, my son, open the door, my love,' my mother pleaded. 'Tell us something. What happened?'

We kept exchanging worried glances. After a while I told her to go into her room and let me speak to him myself. 'Please make him come out,' she pleaded as she left, adding, 'I will offer some nafl prayers to ward off this evil.' I kept knocking on the door, hoping he would open it. I was afraid he might end up doing something to himself.

You see, he was about to get married in three days, and all the preparations were complete. That was his last day of job duty.

After a while, the pauses between his sniffles grew longer and I wasn't sure if I heard anything. I was seriously worried. I finally declared, 'Okay, Akbar, I am going to break in if you don't open the door.' I had been threatening this for some time to no avail but now I felt I had no choice. 'Get out of the door's way, Akbar.'

I rammed my shoulder into the door and it banged open. The steel latch holding the door fell out with its screws and jangled on the floor, the door slammed against the wall. He sat shrivelled under the washbasin.

He was cold blue when I lifted him with his hands and he was shivering as if he'd caught a chill in his bones. (It was sweltering hot outside.) He refused to move out. I called my mother and we forced him to the table where, morsel by morsel and gulp by gulp we made him eat and drink. He wept constantly.

My mother sat beside him, loudly reciting prayers, telling him, 'Acha acha, now, Akbar, my son...that's enough, my child. Recite Alhamdullilah. Recite the kalima, durood... come, my dear, come. Stop, my dear. Stop now.'

I was sitting beside him, holding a glass of water, watching my mother constantly rubbing her hand over his cheeks, and his welled up eyes dripping water. He was in a strange state. His shirt buttons broken as if he had been mourning. Suddenly he said, 'Maa, I held the dead body of a boy today. He was an angel I tell you. An angel.' And started weeping again. We sat there, unsure of what was happening and unable to find a way to handle a grown man weeping incessantly. He then began slapping his forehead with his palm. My mother threw herself at him and I held him from doing so. We let him go when he calmed down. He stretched his hands and stared into them, 'You know his clothes smelled of hashish, but when I touched his body I felt a light inside me. His body was crushed inside a car and he was dead but his wounds were dry, and he was smiling. I touched his forehead and it was cold with sweat. But then, but then...' and he started weeping again. He pulled out a bunch of business cards from his pocket and spread them out on the table beside his plate of food. I picked one up. It smelled of intense black smoke and read: *Chief Security Services. Sadeq Khayyam. Ph #: 0300-xxx-xxxx*

Akbar did not sleep that night. At the call for prayers at dawn, he got up and left for the mosque. My mother saw him leaving and told him not to stay long and come home soon. She thought he would calm down when he prayed. But when he did not return for some time, she woke me up. 'He's gone for more than an hour now. Go see where he is... my heart is troubled. God knows what evil is eating up my child. He was so happy until yesterday... wedding in three days...May God protect us.'

I found him standing at the edge of our lane, staring out onto the main road, the few buses running in the morning, people like shadows ascending them, filling in to go to factories. He got scared when I approached him. Then he recognized me and embraced me. He clung to my body for a long time. He was still shivering from cold. He broke into sobs and said, 'They are here, bhai! They are here! I have seen them walking over the corpses... They are here!' His voice trembled and he shook uncontrollably. Watching him, for a moment I felt scared.

Obviously, when I told this to my mother, we thought he had seen—probably even handled—ripped, mangled bodies, and was traumatized. She gave him a spoonful of

honey from the neighbours to go with some warm milk.
We then sat with him until he went to sleep. My mother
said she wouldn't go to work, 'I will take care of him and
will also get a talisman to ward off his evil.'

That evening when I came home, I was shocked to find
the house in utter silence.

For the past week and a half, each evening was spent
in festivities of dholki—family folks gathered, girls from
the neighbourhood came in and there was lots of singing
and dancing, and the closer we got to the wedding day,
the louder each evening became. I discovered that
when everyone was playing the dhol and singing, Akbar
entered the room enraged, and shouted at everyone,
'Enough! Shut out this singing and dancing! You don't
know—doomsday is here. I have seen them with my
eyes... they are here! Rectify your end! There is no time
left now!'

My mother, poor woman, stared at him with disbelief.
She wanted to have the first marriage in the house with
great fanfare. She had even refused to quit her job until
Akbar got married. She worked in a garments factory,
where she cleaned the fluff that was generated in the
knitting machines. Her work had rapidly destroyed her
lungs and now she regularly spat blood. Her refrain was,
'I'll quit once my Akbar is happily married. I am saving
up for him. I want to have at least a television in the

house when he gets married. What else will I do with my daughter-in-law all day? If we have a television, we would be able to watch good dramas at least.'

It was even worse when the bride-to-be heard about this. She was the daughter of my aunt, my mother's sister. We had all grown up together. She was a lovely girl, very shy, kept to herself, never spoke an unnecessary word. She was a good match for Akbar, much better than she was for me. For a long time everyone said that she was going to be married to me...but I had refused to marry because I wanted to start my own business. I mean, I had a clerical job at the bank but had decided I wanted a successful business before anything else. So I had promised to marry this girl who was the daughter of the owner of a big bakery in our area. She was not good-looking or anything (in fact, quite the opposite) and I felt nothing for her but she was happy with me and ready to convince her family to help me. The deal was done, more or less. I was waiting for my father-in-law to put my business on solid foundations before I married his daughter. I think he saw it too, but like me, he was a practical man. He understood that long-term relationships can only be built on trade and commerce. I felt a little bad about it, but to be honest, that's how life works.

Once my business was up and running, I planned to start a little general store for Akbar. He has that kind of a temperament. I knew he would've been happy with it.

Anyway, my mother was worried when Akbar yelled

at everyone like that. She said, 'I don't know what he has seen and what has come over him...I feel he has some jinn's shadow on him...' Somebody had suggested to my mother that it could be a jinn and that we should go see the Maulvi sahib.

Maulvi sahib lived with his wife and four kids in a single room inside the mosque. He was a very pious man and people from far and wide came to seek his prayers for their ailments. We explained to him what had happened and he looked deeply concerned. He asked us to wait outside his room while he spoke to Akbar himself in private. We could hear Akbar telling him something in a low voice. After a while they grew quiet. Maulvi sahib came out and spoke to us, and he told us the strangest story.

Akbar told him that on the afternoon of the bomb blast, he and his paramedic were lifting the wounded into the ambulance when he saw two men in long pink robes, walking among the dead bodies. They had dirty faces, as if rubbed with charcoal, bald heads, and their tongues were sharp and elongated and hung down to their chins. They were walking over the corpses, touching them, looking joyous and thrilled. Most strangely, no one—not the police, press or anyone else present—was paying attention to them. They roamed freely, and they seemed happy and celebrating. Akbar was convinced that these were Gog and Magog; that they had finally broken free of their thousands of years of wall and were here now; and that they were in this city, the harbingers of the Day of Judgement.

My mother and I looked at each other incredulously. A strange fear cut through both of us.

(If you don't already know about Gog and Magog, their arrival was supposed to mark the coming of the end of the world. Gog and Magog were two leaders of a giant warrior race that had been separated from humans by a wall of iron and lead. With their hands and legs tied, Gog and Magog were condemned to licking the wall all night in order to break it down. Every night they licked the wall down to the thinness of paper; but come morning, the wall replenished itself to its original thickness. They fell asleep with exhaustion and the next night set out to work down the wall again. One of the signs of the Day of Judgement is that the wall will cease to replenish itself and they would manage to bring it down and flee from the prison. They will bring strife and disharmony and, ultimately, the apocalypse to the world.)

Akbar said he had no doubt it was them. He also made repeated mentions of a boy, whose body he pulled out from the rubble. He said that boy was an angel, destined for Heaven. He also told Maulvi sahib that he could not get married—he felt no desire; he felt physically empty; he was just eyesight looking out from his head. He could feel no desire for anything. He said nobody could see what he saw, and there was no way he could say it. He pleaded to him to save him from getting married.

After reporting this, Maulvi sahib turned to my mother and said, 'It is a difficult time, but God is merciful. You keep reciting the prayers I told you last time. Besides that, give some alms. Inshallah, things will get better. And yes, don't get him married. You will destroy the girl's life most of all.'

He was a good man; he consoled us; said the worst was over.

We did not know what to do. The wedding was in two days.

It was then that my mother told me about the dream she had a few days earlier. In her dream she was sleeping when she was awakened by a strong stench of birds. She saw that the house had been invaded by hungry ravens and kites that were tearing apart everything that she had prepared for Akbar's wedding. They were at work quietly at first but when she woke up (as in, woke up in her dream) all the birds began squealing. She saw the floor covered in bird shit and tattered clothes hung from the ceiling fan, and while some birds hovered around the room, a few of them sat in a neat line along the edge of the steel cupboard in the bedroom where most of the wedding stuff was stocked. 'You know the terrifying bit? All of them were looking at me menacingly, as if angry at me for having done something wrong,' she told me breathlessly. 'That image haunts me. I have been reciting ayat-al kursi continuously. When I saw Akbar yelling and kicking today, that's the first thing I thought.'

I cannot tell you what I felt as she told me all this. Up until now, I felt as if we had met an unfortunate accident, but now, suddenly I began feeling something entirely different. As if we were trapped in the middle of a story we did not know, and had no control over.

I felt afraid in a way that I had not been before. On the one hand was my poor brother, who had been cold and silent since that night, and on the other there were omens for us. I also felt that it was possibly my sins that had brought this upon my family.

But really what could we have done? The preparations for the wedding were already made. We had little means, and it had taken us everything to put this wedding together. It was impossible for my mother to postpone or change the wedding date. She was sick with worry. My brother, on the other hand, was in no condition to get married. Then something even stranger happened.

My mother got a call from my aunt saying that the previous night the girl had consumed an overdose of sleeping pills because she wanted to marry somebody else. My aunt was crying and begging apologies but then my mother told her that Akbar had not been feeling well since the bomb blast either and wanted to put off the marriage himself. It was according to God's will. Everything would be fine, they agreed.

Much to our relief, the wedding was called off but it left our home in disarray. My mother's pain was all too visible as she packed or handed away things that she had prepared for Akbar's wedding. Akbar, on the other hand, was a walking mute. He had given up ambulance driving, taken up other jobs and quickly lost each one of them. He now sat at home and did nothing all day. My mother spoke to him, and he replied in his cold, staid manner. She cried and prayed for him.

As far as I was concerned, the shock of those couple of days gradually faded, but more and more I was filled with an intense curiosity to find out about those two men that my brother saw. I wanted to see if they were still in the city. And if what he said was true. It was strange, I realized: I didn't really believe it, but I did not have the courage to disbelieve what my brother saw either.

I went to a friend who had a barbershop in that area. His shop was located in one of the lanes away from the main road where the blast had occurred, but the force of the explosion was such that all the windows and glass in his shop had shattered. 'Yes, we all rushed out to see what had happened, but there was such madness. The ambulances, fire engines all came later. Before that I saw ripped smoking body parts scattered everywhere,' he covered his face with his hand. 'One glance at the scene made me sick. I couldn't take it anymore.' He did not remember seeing two men in pink cloaks.

I spoke to a few more people in the area and most people—to my surprise—actually did see them but nobody had taken any special notice and everybody seemed to be confirming the view that they were garbage collectors, 'or something like it'.

I finally met a young man whose account was close to my brother's. His PCO shop was located right across the site of the blast. He was warm and welcoming. He offered me tea and the only chair in his shop.

'I had my shop's shutter down—I have my lunch and siesta during that hour—when the entire place shook and I thought something has happened and the building was about to fall. I woke up and tried to get out but when I pulled up the shutter it was stuck—look,' he pointed at a hammered edge of the shutter. 'It was such a powerful explosion that the shutter slipped out of its groove. Thank God I don't shut it down completely. I crawled out from this much space and the first thing I saw were these two men in pink cloaks. They were bald men, with dark faces...'

He, too, found it strange that nobody noticed them. He said there was something strange about the way they walked. 'They were like rats, to be honest. They roamed the entire area and nobody was noticing them,' his forehead was tense. 'They had bags and they were picking something up from the rubble. I didn't dare go close to them but I watched them closely. At one point, I felt one of them pause and look straight at me over the crowd, and even from this distance I felt they radiated the blackest energy.'

As he spoke, I felt a coldness overtake me. He said he didn't stay there and rushed home. 'But you know the really funny thing,' he said gravely, 'I saw them again the next day, and then again the day after. I followed them and found out they live in an apartment just two lanes behind ours.' He pointed his thumb over his shoulder. 'But obviously I never had the courage to go and see what they were all about. To be honest, I am just scared.' Then he paused and said, 'If you go to see them, I will go with you.'

We made inquiries and found out that those two strange 'creatures' in pink clothes (that's how people referred to them)—their heads identically shrunk and deformed, and their tongues hanging out from their mouths—lived with a freak who was a painter and did palmistry for a living. 'All of them are into this shady business; nobody knows what they do,' the man who fried samosas below the apartment building told us. 'They get some interesting visitors though,' he winked and laughed. We did not know what he meant.

The apartment staircase smelled of urine. It was dimly lit by the light coming through the air vent. On the fifth floor, we rang the bell and waited. A few moments later, we heard a clank of metal followed by a man's feeble voice, 'Is that you? Why so late? The door's open.'

The PCO boy turned the knob and in front of us stood a middle-aged man with a large bird cage in front of him. He looked at us for a moment and instead of showing any surprise, he turned away. 'Give me two minutes,' he said, and inserted his hand into the cage.

From inside the cage, he pulled out a large kite that screeched as it hopped on his arm; he petted it on the head and brought his face near its head and whispered something. 'This one needs a lot of attention,' he smiled. 'She's wild, but okay, really. If I don't attend to her, she will scream and not let us speak,' he said, as he caressed the back of the kite's ferocious head. The air in the room was saturated with the stench of the bird. We watched him as he kept whispering to the bird, petting it, smiling all the time. He then put it back inside the cage and from his shirt-pocket pulled out a pair of dark glasses and put them on. We were still standing at the door.

He took us inside a room filled with painting canvases. I sat facing the canvas on the easel. I was immediately drawn in by the almost-finished painting, which showed a bunch of demons running around toward a naked woman who was smirking at the audience. 'She's a sorceress,' he said to me. 'They are all running crazy because she is so beautiful. Ah, look at her. Isn't she just *beautiful*?' he smiled and looked admiringly at the woman. 'Yes, she knows it too. But nobody can touch her because she is more powerful than all of them. But her problem is that if she makes love to them, she loses her invincibility and they will tear her apart. Everybody's miserable here,' he laughed. 'You understand?'

I nodded, not sure what was going on.

'Now tell me, are you looking for any specific information about your future? You know my rates? Five hundred for the first session where I only read your hand. A thousand for the second session, I'll get to know you better and we'll do some astrology too. Third session I charge two thousand and we use palmistry, astrology and numerology. All information would be correct. Guaranteed. Now who wants to go first, you?' he pointed to the PCO boy.

I explained to him the situation. I told him that my brother and the PCO boy had seen the two men at the site of the blast and we were looking for them. Did he know them?

'Ah, those two. I don't know them. I don't. But they were living here until last week, but now they have left. I do not know anything about them, actually. I saw them rummaging through garbage at four in the morning last week—you know, I go out to feed meat to the kites of this city, and it is unusual to find garbage collectors at that time—I understood immediately that they weren't garbage collectors, so I thought they must be looking for food, so I brought them home and gave them food, and they stayed here for some days. But then they started getting in the way of my work and I told them to get the hell out of here. They were strange, yes,' he said as his voice wandered around in lower tones, and he began speaking to himself. 'You know I bring such people home, because it keeps prying eyes away from this place. But Gog Magog, you say, end of the world you mean, strange you bring that up, very strange.'

He then took off his glasses and wiped them. His eyelids were fluttering rapidly.

'You see,' he said, 'I cannot see anything more than a few feet; my eyes are bad. I stay in this place most of the time; I go out early in the morning to give meat to kites and in the afternoon I feed pigeons in my balcony. That day, not one pigeon came down. Strange you say, yes? That day I was wondering about the birds—why they were in a frenzy, screeching madly and circling the skies non-stop. I sat there and felt their cacophony was rising, but nobody was paying any attention. Just around the time of the bomb blast, I started feeling that I would go mad. And when that blast happened, I truly felt the world had come to an end. I stood in my balcony, smelling a dark unforgiving burning smell and understood what it must be like in Hell where everything evil burns together,' he sighed. 'And then I realized from the smell that there must be birds burning down there too. Although my eyes are bad but I could sense that the birds had collapsed and had fallen into that acid mix of things on the ground. That's when I rushed in and told those two boys to run down and fill their sacks with all the birds they could find so that I could bury them properly.' Here his tone became graver. 'You know, I cannot see animals suffer. It's terrible.

'I stood in my balcony after the blast—for how long I don't know, maybe an hour, maybe two hours—for a long time—and then I started hearing sounds. I heard sea waves crashing, squeals of creatures of the sea that I am sure nobody has heard or seen before. I wasn't the only person who heard them. A lot of people hear these things but they ignore them because that's not how they understand things. That entire day and next, I heard a loud crane-like sound coming from the sea. I knew monsters were heading this way. The sound was so overwhelming that my eyes watered and hands trembled with fear and I couldn't even talk. And what happens the next day? They found that 40-foot whale dead on the beach. I don't know why you say they were Gog and Magog but I can tell you that this city is dying. Look around yourself: do you see anything that might tell you it is living? All the birds are leaving this city. Soon we will only have crows and rats left in this city.'

Just then we heard the door open and heard the rustling of a dress. He called out, 'Is that you? I can smell you. Come here.'

A woman in a burqa with strikingly beautiful eyes peeked into the room. She was about to take off her veil and headscarf. She paused when she saw us. 'You have guests? You should have told me,' she sounded irritated.

'Don't be a nuisance, come here, they are nice people.

Not like those... Come here, see I have finished making your painting, come, have a look.'

'Is it done?' her tone changed, as she moved closer to the painting and started examining the nude figure. 'What! My eyes aren't that big!'

'Sorry for that, but is the rest okay?' he said and laughed impishly.

'Hmm. I am in the other room,' she turned around and walked past us, leaving a strong whiff of perfume behind.

The man laughed again.

What appears strange and complex becomes even stranger and more complicated once you begin to investigate it. That's the true nature of the world.

That encounter with that palmist/painter left me with no desire to work or do anything else. For days, I could not concentrate on my work. I began seeing what he meant: this city was dying, this world was ending. All the signs were there for me to see. He was right. I could see it. I began looking around myself and saw that everything was indicating death.

I could not concentrate on my work any more, and my business began to falter. I sold it off before it sank completely. I also lost interest in the baker's daughter. Initially she was puzzled but her enthusiasm also waned and when another marriage proposal came her way, she got married quickly. It was all for the best, thank God.

With the money that was left, I started a little general store in our lane, which now provides our family with enough money to live without any luxuries. Akbar doesn't take interest in the work; he simply sits on his chair behind the store counter, letting the neighbourhood kids steal things from the store. He's also unable to do any serious mental work, and I have to manage everything in the store on my own.

This string of events I have recounted has left me with a belief that we are indeed at the end of the world. I am only waiting for it to happen now; indeed, preparing for it. Normally, one would imagine that such a conviction would lead to despair, but strangely enough, instead of despair, I feel liberated. I feel lighter since I have resigned myself to live this way—without ambition or greed of money or anything. I think a lot about my life now, something I had never done, I realize, because earlier my ambition did not allow me to be honest with myself about what I was doing and what it was doing to me. Now I feel free to admit to everything I have done in my life and see things with a clear eye. I feel free to repent without needing to cover up anything. Every day I feel gratitude that God has created ways for us to repent; told us how to make up for our wrongdoings. I give alms, I pray, and try hardest to live my life honestly as much as possible. It's not easy to live this way because every day I find my memory throws up more vile things I have done in the past. Each day there is a new guilt for me to deal with. I spend my life making up for everything I have done wrong.

What weighs on me still, however, is the condition of my brother. I still find it difficult to look at him. My only prayer to God is for his revival; I want him to live life with the same zest that he had before that fateful day, no matter if it is the end of the world.

Maps of a New City

Look again at the bullet-smashed screen: the bullet hole is a new territory. It cracks new paths, new boundaries.

These are maps of an uncharted city. They tell different stories.

Listen.

A WRITER IN THE CITY

Things and Reasons

I WAS EDITING AN obscure story on unexplored copper reserves somewhere in Balochistan when I caught snatches of unwanted dialogue volleying across the newsroom ('Cantt Station!' 'platform? platform?' 'how many people?' 'the intersection?' 'in the railway carriage? platform?' 'no, no, outside' 'yes, yes,' 'outside the station, on the chowk!' 'at the intersection!' 'how many people?'). I did not pay attention. I wanted nothing more than to finish editing the story and then have my tea before leaving office.

My final cup of tea is my daily salvation. I have it alone in the empty conference room staring into the wall in front of me with my back toward the office. It's a kind of daily meditation. My mind goes headlong into a free fall that lasts approximately for the duration of my cup of tea. Those few vacant minutes are the most gratifying of my entire work day. They settle the heat and dust of the day, and by the time I reach the sugar at the bottom of the cup (I don't stir my tea) I am feeling a glorious emptiness. It's what contentment for me feels like. That day I took leave early, and found myself in the conference room a couple of hours earlier. It was still afternoon and I was looping the string of the steaming teabag around the teaspoon when the phone started to ring. I ignored it. But it rang again.

And again.

Finally, I picked it up. It was for me (somebody must have told the operator I was in the conference room). They wanted to know if I knew somebody called Sadeq because he had had a bad accident and they had found my number in his wallet.

'Is he okay?' I asked, staring into my tea.

'Come to Jinnah Hospital immediately. He was in a car when the blast happened.'

Pause.

'Are you coming?'

'Yes,' I stood up.

I waited for a few seconds then sat down. I picked up the teaspoon strapped with the teabag and dripped it over a bunch of ants walking on the table.

For the next fifty seconds I stared at the wall. I sat down again and watched the dead ants floating on the smoking brown liquid.

The security wardens at the hospital were busy pushing people as politely as they could to keep them from crowding the hospital gate. Ambulances were racked up behind each other, and the ambulance drivers were plugged into the megaphones: *Get out of the way! Get out of the way! Make way for the ambulance! Get out of the way!* Some drivers were more specific: *You, red shirt! Make way! Amma ji, don't walk in front of the ambulance! Get out of the way!*

I waved my press card at the security warden and he let me pass. Inside the hospital building, I was pointed to a man behind the counter who was chewing betel leaf and had a calm look on his face. He had a register of all the patients who had been identified so far.

He traced his finger down to Sadeq's name and turned the register around pointing at a scribbled name, next to #09. I read the name and for a moment felt the ground move physically. He asked me if I was the patient's brother. I shook my head.

Then on the register I saw another name I knew. I pointed to #54, 'Is he also dead?'

'Hmm… yes.' He saw my face and pointed his thumb over his shoulder. 'No use going inside right now. You won't find them. Wait outside.'

I ignored him and went inside the emergency ward. End to end, the room was packed with stretchers and beds that were heaped with patients. There was hardly any room to move between the beds and stretchers. Doctors surrounded by assistants, nurses, paramedics were busy firefighting—yelling out instructions and instrument names. Right in front of me, a naked man was held by three medics in a sitting position; his skin had been shaved off his body for the most part. His mouth was open and he was droning a constant guttural rasp.

'How do we get him to quiet down?' asked one of the assistants from the senior doctor, an old man in a kurta shalwar, who was working with his sleeves rolled up and with a silver wristwatch jangling on his arm. 'Let him be. The vibration of his voice relaxes his nerves and numbs his pain,' he replied. 'Natural painkiller.'

I felt nauseated. I went outside to the parking area for air.

The parking area too was in a state of panic. The family, friends and relatives of the injured were clamouring outside the hospital gates. I was among the earliest to arrive. Then something bizarre caught my eye. In front of the ambulances, a boy was slapping his forehead with his palm. His shirt was torn and his face looked bruised, as if he had been in a fight. At first I thought he was one of the mourning relatives but then I noticed his ID slung around his neck and realized he was an ambulance driver.

'Akbar! Oye, Akbar! Give a hand here.' Behind him, another paramedic was hollering out to him, as he tried to pull out a woman from the ambulance. The woman being pulled out was already dead but I could sense a movement in her body—she was alive the same way flesh is warm after death, alive to pain and sensation. Akbar did not hear his friend; instead, he started walking like he was in a trance: his head penduluming from side to side, his eyes fixed to the ground. He walked headfirst into the iron gate of the hospital and banged it hard. The collision woke him up. The security warden standing nearby shook him by his shoulder, 'Oye you, boy, you okay? You need water or something? Don't stand here.'

~

A hot cloud of dust and exhaust was billowing around my face. The air was filled with the refracted heat of the late sun. I was walking on the Clifton bridge.

My eyes were following the blue plastic bag that floated in between the onrushing cars. It curved sideways, rose and cruised and hung in the air, and finally ran into the path of a pedestrian who slapped it with the back of his hand and pushed it over the edge of the bridge. It limped over it and spiralled like a tiny tornado.

I was feeling a disconnect in my body, which was beating to a much slower rhythm than my mind. Somebody at the hospital said that the bomb went off just outside the station, at the intersection. In my mind I was seeing that triangular intersection where at this time of the day the traffic locked into each other because one lane was blocked by buses that treated it as a five-minute stop. The buildings around the intersection were marked with permanent cracks that showed how this city had aged over the decades, having withstood the incessant assault of noise, smoke and dust.

In my memory, I looked hard at them, but I couldn't

understand what they meant. Along the street-level, I was reading signs outside old establishments offering cheap and dirty stays to travellers and residents—I paused to look at one that offered haircuts, steam baths and massage. A few metres ahead, a crowd was gathered around the intra-city bus terminal; people were piling on top of the roofs of the buses because all seats were taken. In the apartment building just above the bus terminal, a man's thick arms hung out of the railings of his third-floor balcony. He wore a vest and shalwar and he was yelling to a man below who was waving something in his hand. Beside the man in the vest, a woman was hanging clothes on the clothesline.

The other name I had read on the register of the dead at the hospital was Comrade Sukhansaz. He was one of my father's dearest friends and a man I had known since I was a child. It occurred to me that his family also lived in one of the apartments adjacent to Cantt Station. Was he on his way to meet his family when the blast happened? Was he leaving? Did he come and decide it was not a good idea to meet them? He used to say to my father that marriage was his biggest comfort and his biggest mistake. After his son was born, he said, he had started feeling alienated from his work, to which he had dedicated his life. He cared only about his son. Nothing else was important to him any more. 'That scared me,' he said, 'and I realized it had to be one thing: family or revolution. But a man is allowed only one irreparable

170

mistake in his life—then at least he can work his life out so as to justify the mistake. But I made two. Having a child was a mistake because of my work. And when my son was born, I realized committing to my work was a mistake. You know what Gautama said? *There are only two mistakes one can make along the road to Truth: Not going all the way, and not starting.* I think I made both. Two mistakes make a man blind. You lose your ability to see and understand things. You go mad. Mad.'

I was standing somewhere near where the curve of the bridge peaked. The sky from the bridge looked a white metal sheet. This bridge was one of the few places I visited often. On this bridge, the world made sense, even if momentarily. I had spent many hot afternoons standing here, feeling the feral breeze of this city, and staring at the railway tracks forking below—abandoned and alone for miles, and watching the kites scout the skies overhead, and pigeons, crows and sparrows beneath them, all pursuing their always scramble. On the bridge you could stand aside, and simply observe the enormous angry mad busy world rushing past you.

I began dreaming of Sadeq with whom I had spent most evenings during the last three years, listening to his daily digest of car recovery stories, his musings on love, his weird descriptions of people and places in his angry, funny, doped up voice. We were friends in school who lost each other afterward but then we rediscovered our friendship after college.

Back in the school, we hunted as a pair. I had a sharp tongue and he was a bully, full of untamed flair. But during the years of his absence he had turned into a hard, vengeful spirit who revelled in the fear and intimidation he caused. He said he cared very little for the world. But the truth was different. He was running away from things he loved. (In that sense we were alike.) In his crooked messy way he did love people. And in his way, he found that love reciprocated too. But he hated himself for being a criminal. He once told me about an old man he helped outside a hospital and how holding his frail body sickened him. How he tried not to think of that man because it made him sick of what he was doing every day of his life and how he lived. Those were rare moments though when he lowered his guard. I remember once while playing hooky from school, we ran into some policemen who harassed him and he broke down. We never spoke about that incident but I believed that was the moment we became friends.

My mind drifts. I was dreaming of that café at Cantt Station where I went looking for an old man we had met on the bus on that trip—the old writer, the truant, who roved the city and wrote stories about all the truants of this city. The café he told me about was adjacent to the intersection. It was a Persian café that served cheap food and tea and fruitcakes; its dark hall was packed with booths that had wooden furniture and tables with marble-tops. The incubated air inside smelled fuzzy—frying things mixing with car fumes wafting in from the street; its darkness diffused with white tubelights. For a while, in my mind, I was there again, listening to the din and tumble of life inside the café.

Out at the street, I saw a boy in a car with a girl stuck in the traffic jam. It reminded me of a story a friend once told me of a botched date where he got stuck in the Cantt Station traffic, and by the time he managed to extricate himself from it, it was time for the girl to return home.

These stories, I realized, were lost. Nobody was going to know that part of the city but as a place where a bomb went off. The bomb was going to become the story of this city. That's how we lose the city—that's how our knowledge of what the world is is taken away from us—when what we know is blasted into rubble and what is created in its place bears no resemblance to what there was and we are left strangers in a place we knew, in a place we ought to have known. Suddenly, it struck me that that's how my father experienced this city. How, when he walked this city, he was tracing paths from his memory to the present—from what this place had been to what it had become.

My mind now was a hard knotted skein of voices of the two men I had lost. I could hear their voices in my head: both of them raucous, loud, foul-mouthed. But beneath their cacophony of noises I could sense the menacing silence of their deaths. I felt as if my heart had been violently torn out of its cage and all its pieces flung into the world. My forehead was cold with sweat.

As I walked down the bridge, I saw a car windscreen lying on the footpath. It was battered with bullet holes. I stopped and examined it. It was an absurd thing to be lying on a footpath. I stood looking at the sharp, clean webs around the bullet holes. A stunningly violent, shockingly beautiful object—a crass memento of this city to mark this moment.

I walked down the bridge to climb the first bus I could get—to be somewhere else.

Things go on.

~

I do not remember when was the last time I strayed from the path I followed from my apartment to work and back. But I do remember very well how and why it was established.

There came a point in my life when I started looking for a job with a hard, inflexible routine. I started searching for work that would help me get away from writing; work that would not leave me with a craving to reach for words because here's the thing: writing was an inescapable torture for me. I could not do it, yet it was the only thing I desperately wanted to do.

I had tried many things to effect my escape—worked as a sales person for car tyres; a receptionist; a signboard painter; plumber; cotton-filler for pillows and quilt covers; an overseer in a garment factory—but when I came home at the end of each day, I reached for pen and paper and wrote down the little fragments that filled my head. I wandered the city for hours—I hung about the old markets, sat at the rickshaw and taxi stands, observed alleged criminals around the city courts, ogled at customers buying condoms and electronic gadgets and spices and haggling over meat and used books and parrots—and each day, I came home brimming with the manic psychic energy of the city, with countless nameless voices in my head, and tried to write it all. But nothing I wrote was up to the task of capturing this ruinously mad city. Each day was another exercise in despair.

But that wandering the streets, to be honest, was also just another search for how to look away. I wanted to forget—because, like everyone, I had a lot to forget: I wanted to forget my father and his stories that were of no use to me but that nonetheless haunted me and interrupted my life and imagination and my writing. I wanted to purge myself of his imagination. I wanted to write against his idea of stories. I wanted to write stories that were completely unlike his stories—ones that had *no* element of fabrication. I wanted the voices on the page to be as true as the ones I heard. But as I wrote, I gradually realized that there was nothing called true stories. Only fragments were true.

So I wrote in fragments. My fragments were things as I saw them. Things as they were—I wrote as intensely as I saw and heard and felt but all the fragments I wrote had a hole in the centre where life was supposed to be. All of them were meaningless. I wrote reams but the more I wrote the more I felt I was sinking deeper, each time ever more hopelessly, into the quicksand of my own little islands while the universe moved past me at its own indifferent pace.

That's when I found this job as the sub-editor in a newspaper office, and it salvaged me from this despair. I spent my six hours in the news office, sub-editing the files of raw reported stories that were placed in my computer folder. The work itself was insipid, and most days left me with a stiff headache. But what made it tolerable— even pleasant, occasionally—was the continual relief of completing small tasks that punctuated the day. At the end of the day, my cup of tea waited for me. After that I headed home, where I'd spend a couple of hours drinking quality whisky with Sadeq, and around seven, we'd go down to the dhaba to dine on tea and parathas.

That had been my schedule for the last three years and my release from the oppressiveness of writing. (Although it left me with a disgusting sense of loneliness, but that's a different matter.) This job had suitably shrunk my universe to myself—and the city had been reduced into a few roads that I traversed to and from work without paying any attention to my surroundings. I stopped roving the city too.

So when I received the phone call asking me to get to the hospital, I worried about Sadeq but to be honest my first reaction was resentfulness for the fact that this bit of news threw me off my daily routine. I had to walk again on roads I had not walked in years now. It made me nervous.

~

The bus beat rambunctiously with the jhankar versions of old Bollywood numbers as it moved slowly and aggressively through the viscous traffic. It pressed down upon smaller vehicles like a big-chested bully who knew precisely how to execute its mass and noise into movement: it froze the traffic with a sudden burst of a honk and then—with a growl of the engine and the spit of the exhaust—thrust its snout into the gap that opened up between the slow-moving traffic. It pushed forward until the rear fitted snugly one spot ahead.

Across the aisle, a little boy was sitting with his father. He wore a red Coca Cola cap (too large for his head). His father was explaining to him the dangers of the bus driver's irresponsible aggression, 'One wrong move, the bus is going to scratch the side of some car, and these people will break into a fight, and we'll be stuck here. We are already late. Everybody is waiting for us at your phuppo's place.' I watched the little boy as he clasped the seat in front of him with his little hands and absorbed his father's anxieties. His father poked his head out of the window and looked ahead, and then shook his head. 'Okay, what was that game you taught me? Rock-paper-what? Let's play that.'

When I was a kid, I played a game with my father called Blackboards. We closed our eyes and suggested to each other various things that we drew on the blackboards we imagined in our heads. It was a game I used to learn spellings. My first lessons as a writer. I closed my eyes and saw the blackboard again—only for it to vanish and my mind to be flooded with images of the hospital: the man with the guttural voice held down by the medics; that ambulance boy, Akbar.

Living in this city, you developed a certain relationship with violence and news of violence: you expected it, dreaded it, and then when it happened, you worked hard to look away from it, because there was nothing you could do about it—not even grieve, because you knew that it will happen again and maybe in a way that was worse than before. Grieving is possible only when you know you have come to an end, when there is nothing more to follow. This city was full of bottled-up grief.

It took a moment for me to realize I was the same in some sense. I had not yet grieved for my father.

My father was a writer of stories for children who gave up writing to become a street performer. He was haunted by nightmares. During the Zia-ul-Haq years, he had spent a fortnight in jail where he watched his friends get tortured. (For writers and members of the intelligentsia they favoured torture methods that did not leave body marks.

They force-fed them, and did not allow them to either sleep or relieve themselves. By the end of the second day, most were ready to renounce their causes along with their kids and wives and all else that lies in between.) He had dreams about that time in jail and they kept getting worse as he grew older. During the long period after he lost his job, the city was racked with violence, his nightmares turned worse too. He began fearing sleep. He wanted an escape, so he gave up writing and took up an apprenticeship with a street magician, and soon he was popping live chicks from tennis balls while performing for children across poorer neighbourhoods in the city for petty change that people spared.

My father met Comrade Sukhansaz in jail, and they remained friends till my father's death. They spent long hours together speaking of days past and I sat by them overhearing their conversations. I never got the references and names they exchanged, but they shared a deep love for this city and I always sensed their conversations had a set pattern: an initial animation winding down into an abiding sadness.

I got off the bus at the Empress Market stop. It had been years since I had last been here but no matter the time of the day, this junction was a full throat: a two-lane road with one lane encroached by street hawkers. This was also the patch of road where bus drivers left their buses in the middle of the road and went searching for some corner to piss.

I almost lost my balance as I squeezed myself out of the rear door crammed with men. If getting on the bus was a struggle, getting off a running bus was a downright challenge to survival. You risked your limbs at the least and falling flat on your face at the most. Only years of riding experience prepared you in the abrasive art of negotiating them. (To get on the bus you must be visible to the bus driver speeding at you. Wave at him. He will slow down if you're a man, slow down very much if you are a lucky man, but he will halt completely only for women, especially older ones. So if you're a man, which you were, run and try to be in front of others running with you. Catch hold of the side bars first, keep running, put one foot on the pedestal, and pull yourself up. There—you're off the ground and on the bus. To get off the bus, get to the rear door at least fifteen seconds before you want to get off and bang the steel door. Hit it hard. Make sure the driver hears the bang. If not, bang again. At all events, make sure the conductor hears the bang. He will be around somewhere, collecting fares, trying to adjust people to make room for one more person in there. If he hears you banging wildly, he will whistle the special whistle and the bus driver will slow down. This is also called stopping. Also remember: the bus driver doesn't care how you get off—or if you get off. The banging on the steel door—that must stop. Get off now.)

I disentangled myself from the mass of people and leaped out from the rear door, and stumbled as I landed on the road.

'Look out, bhayya!'—a hand grabbed my arm and helped steady me. I thanked the man, who replied, smiling, 'I usually charge a fee for such help, you know...'

A crowd was building up next to a small cart selling fried innards of assorted animals, releasing a putrid smell. I went closer to the crowd and tried to glance over the huddle. 'Look at that dagger!' was the whisper going around. 'Look at that *thing* in his neck!' Ah, the dagger: a full foot-long—at least. Half of it on either side of his neck. 'Look, the damn thing even *looks* real!' someone exclaimed again in a whisper.

He was a stick of a man with a dagger going through his neck. Dressed in a pink tattered cloak, he was singing at the top of his voice:

I am the bird of death
I have come back from the Land of the Dead
To tell you...

He had a round face, a thin neck, and his facial expressions were deeply crumpled, as though he was in great pain. His eyes were looking straight ahead at no one in particular and he held a large cardboard to his chest and was singing at the top of his voice:

I am the bird of death
I have come back from the Land of the Dead
To tell you...

I looked around to see the people watching this—half-believing, half-amused.

Friends: My brother was a soldier. Once he was passing by a graveyard while returning from his duty when he heard terrifying cries that would burst open your head. When he went inside, what he saw was nothing short of hell on earth: a little, rat-like animal, red eyes, white fur, was sitting on a pile of bones. When that animal with his venomous teeth struck at the bones, they let out excruciating screams. They were screams the likes of which my brother had heard neither in war nor in torture. He wanted to save the dead man's soul from this torture of the grave.

So he took out his gun and shot at the little rat-like animal. Next thing he knew, the creature was running after him. He ran as fast as he could and finally, when he came across a pond of water, jumped in to save himself. Now listen to this and find lessons for your salvation: that creature stopped just short of the pond. My brother thought he was saved. The animal took a mouthful of water and spat it back into the pond. My friends, the water of the pond turned into acid. I swear. The body of my brother became witness to it. He

*lost his body from his chest down. It was burnt with
an acid which has no cure. The government of Pakistan
has shown him to all kinds of doctors, but no one
understands the burns or the cure. This is his picture...*

He then turned around the cardboard he was holding to
his chest and we all witnessed a collage of black and white
pictures of horribly scarred arms and back. The crowd fell
into a hush. Men looked around searching each others'
faces for clues about how to react.

*...if any one of you, respected brothers or friends,
still doesn't believe me, or has doubts, he is welcome
to come with me and visit my brother and ask him to
pray for him. Because God put him through such a
misfortune, his prayers are heard and people find their
heart's desires through his means. If you cannot come
along and still wish to benefit, here is some water that
he has prayed on. It will cure all kinds of pains and
aches. Five rupees each bottle...*

I wasn't sure what to make of it but in a strange
way I felt an affinity toward him. He reminded me of
something—something I did not wish to think about. I
kept watching him from a distance as the crowd thinned
out. He sat on his haunches, carefully removing the two
pieces of the dangling dagger from the sides of his neck.
I stepped closer. He continued to wipe his neck and face

with a little white towel, which had turned crimson with the goo he had pasted all around his neck. He threw the towel on the road, and stood up.

'I want to see your brother. I am a news reporter. I have to interview him and ask him for some prayers,' I said all this in a rush of breath and immediately realized my mistake.

'Mash'allah,' he smiled welcomingly. God has willed it. And then, putting his finger inside his mouth to pick his teeth, he asked, 'You want to come with me now?'

But I did not wish to go. I wanted to be home, to be in my apartment. To be away from this man. From this feeling of knowing him.

My father was particularly fond of stories from the long epic fantasy, *Tilism Hoshruba*. In those stories about evil sorcerers and good tricksters, when a sorcerer was killed, his head would split open and a bird would spring out announcing the sorcerer's name and the murderer's name one by one. 'In this city, a part of us dies each day, and a bird springs out of our open skulls each day announcing our deaths and the addresses of our murderers,' he said to me once while we were taking a walk on the beach, 'but nobody listens. The air is thick with the chorus of these birds of death. Listen.'

My father imagined the world and each object as part of continuous stories. In his stories the universe answered his questions, the past was visible and the future illuminated. Things had reasons and they all connected.

But unlike my father, when I looked back into the past, all I saw was pitch black darkness and heard unnamed voices trying to override each other in their attempts to reach me—and I felt indifferent to all of them. That's when I concluded that my father's way of imagining the universe was naïve, simplistic, and wrong, just plain wrong. He was wrong about the world. The world and its stories did not continue or cohere. We were all just broken parts and so were our stories. True stories are fragments. Anything longer is a lie, a fabrication.

But now, faced with the Bird of Death, I felt as if one of my father's fabrications had come alive and I was in the middle of one of his stories. I had no choice but to follow.

∼

I followed the Bird of Death through the ballooning mass of men, watching the hem of his pink cloak drag along the road. He seemed to be in a hurry and at the back of my mind I was evaluating the sorts of risks this sort of journey entailed.

I felt awkward being in this part of the city. I was back here again after years, in the ferocious noise on the street. Everything around me was shouting—the vendors, the car horns, the rickshaws—even ordinary things hollered, 'Watch where you're going!' The leaning telephone pole yelled at you if you stepped too close to it. Everything could hurt. Insulation was the most important lesson you learned on Karachi's roads: See as little as possible, hear even less, and touch absolutely nothing. Half the trick to surviving here was to learn to extricate yourself from all the invasive influences around you while keeping a calm appearance. The other half was to emanate some of those influences, so that strangers would stay away.

I followed him onto a bus where we took the bench seat right at the back. The ever-open rear door was the only major source of ventilation apart from the jammed plastic windows.

The conductor stood at the rear-gate of the bus, shouting out the names of the stops the bus would make: *Nayee Karachi number teen, Kharadar, Meethadar, Ta, Ta, Ta, Ta…* (Ta, the short form for 'Tower', which is the short form for 'Mereweather Tower'. This is the other rule of this city—fit things to your need, even if it's a name. Borrow someone's finger and make it your screwdriver.)

Finally, the bus moved, like a giant turning in his sleep, and as soon as it gained a few inches, the conductor was upon us. He pointed the bundle of sweaty notes in his hand at me, 'Yes brother, where do you want to go?' I took out the change and turned toward the Bird of Death to ask him for our destination, who said, 'He's with me.' The conductor took the money from him and moved on. We exchanged smiles. 'You didn't have to do this, you know,' I said.

'No, no. You are our guest today. Please,' he smiled. I

was startled by the change in tone. It was an honest smile.

'So... is this all you do? Help your brother?' I asked him after an uneasy pause.

'No, I have other jobs too,' he smiled.

'What do you do?' I asked, but he didn't hear me. He was eyeing something outside the door. He winked at me, 'Watch what I do now.'

He slid off the seat and went over to the open rear door and waved wildly to a young kid selling newspapers on the road. The kid dodged traffic and ran toward the moving bus, holding out a paper, shouting, 'Which one, which one do you want?'

'Not the paper, boy! I want to know the latest news! Tell me the *latest* news!' the Bird of Death shouted back.

The boy had reached very close to the bus when he got the joke. His face flushed with anger and he stopped dead in his tracks and yelled at the top of his voice, 'YOUR MOTHER IS BEING FUCKED ON THAT ROAD OVER THERE! THAT'S THE LATEST NEWS! YOU UNDERSTAND, YOU MOTHERFUCKER?'

The bus gained speed and he just stood at the gate waving his fist at the kid, 'Stay here you bastard! Stay here! Tomorrow I will come and fuck you! Just wait! I will come for you tomorrow!'

When he returned to the seat, judging from his face, I realized it would be impossible to continue speaking to him. Then he unzipped his bag and I saw a gun lying on top of his other paraphernalia.

'Listen, can we do this interview later? Next week, maybe?' I asked after a few minutes had lapsed.

'No,' he replied without even looking at me. 'Do it now. I have come here only for you. You do it now. I have informed them. They are waiting.' Then he suddenly turned to me. 'Show me your ID card again,' and then reading my face, he moved closer and said in a lower voice. 'Show me. I have a weapon. You saw, right?'

I handed him my ID, which read: Reporter/Sub-Editor. (I was only a sub-editor but they always added an extra designation, in case they fired somebody and needed a quick replacement.) 'Hmm, yes, it looks fine,' and then he pocketed my ID. 'I'll keep this as security,' he smiled. 'Just do your work and we'll be fine.'

They say everybody in Karachi has their own crime story: people were looted and beaten up on the streets, inside banks, in their offices and homes, on buses, in cars and restaurants and cafés, but I was in a unique position where I was accompanying the criminal to his preferred spot. None of my father's stories had bastards like this one.

We sat together in silence, without even exchanging glances. He was looking out through the open door. After about twenty minutes, he stood up and banged the door. The bus slowed down and we got off. So this was where it would be: in a squatter settlement. He turned to me, 'Just be respectful. Don't ask too many questions. Listen to the answers carefully and don't question a question. Also, don't ask too many questions.'

~

He was walking briskly ahead of me, almost unmindful of me following him. For somebody holding me at gunpoint, technically speaking, he was doing a pretty poor job. But I think both of us knew that it was his area and I would not try to run away, so I just tried to pay attention to the maze we were in, making mental notes of things I could remember in case I had to find my own way back. As we went further, the lanes became narrower, houses turned into shabbier huts made from an assortment of tattered jackets, old bedsheets, wooden lattices, plastic nets, bamboos tied with plastic bags. It seemed almost impossible how they were a single construction, growing out of each other's backs and fronts. They all seemed knotted at each other's torsos and one wrong move could undo a whole row of houses.

Officially speaking, I was nowhere. This place did not exist. A million people here didn't actually exist on state record; hence this place had no official source of water or sewage lines. People dug their own holes and installed hand-pumps that drew undrinkable water. The children lived and played in garbage heaps and died of common fevers and mosquito bites.

Settlements such as this one bleeped on the radar of the city only when an 'operation' was underway against a criminal gang located there. These places supplied cheap labour for this city's large industry and the majority of its domestic servants. And yet, most people in the 'civilized' parts of this city would have never visited a settlement such as this one. It was the long dark shadow of their city they chose to ignore.

He turned into a broad lane and we stood facing a solid cement and brick house. My sandals by now were covered in the dark thick stinking slime and I could feel the sticky thing even on my feet. The place smelled exactly like a garbage dump.

There was a long queue outside the house, mostly women, standing and squatting in the heat.

We entered the house through a back door, which was hidden behind a pile of trash. We climbed up a narrow staircase and as we stepped into a room, the stink entirely disappeared. 'Wait,' he instructed.

He went behind the curtain, and reappeared in a couple of minutes. 'Just remember what I said: don't ask too many questions,' he cautioned me once more as he parted the curtain for me.

It was a large room littered with charpoys—at least six of them—with dirty cyan walls, and on one side, in a TV-trolley-like box, sat the dark head of a man with a big, silent smile and a thorough gaze. He was just shoulders and head. In a box. A giant head. On giant shoulders. Below the shoulders his body was concealed in a box from his chest downwards. It was a box with wheels. Little box. About two-thirds the size of what his torso would be if he had one...

His naked, scarred hands gathered food from a plate set in front of him. The skin on the visible part of his body and hands seemed like shrivelled pieces of desiccated, parched mud. His face was healthy with well-cut, oiled hair combed to the side, and a neat, dark and dense beard. His palms showed mutilated stumps instead of fingers of different lengths; the thumb seemed like the only surviving tree in that thicket. He dipped his fingers in a plate of rice and lentils and consolidated the contents into a lump, which the thumb deftly gripped and the hand brought to the mouth.

As he chewed his food, he glanced at me only once and smiled. 'Please join me,' he offered, pointing to his plate.

I don't remember what I said, but I refused. Politely, I think.

Luminous—I loathe the word, but there is no other word to describe his eyes—intensely *luminous*. In that room, I felt I was in a presence.

He finished the food and then lifted his plate and wiped it patiently with his thumb. He then licked the thumb. Gradually, he rubbed the plate spotless. He then gestured

191

to the servant standing behind him. I noticed how tightly and neatly his body fitted the box. The servant brought a bowl of water in which he dipped his fingers as he recited a prayer. He was then presented with a small, white towel with which he dried his hands.

All this while he did not look at me.

Finally he turned to me and smiled, 'Salam, my friend.'

I returned his greeting, which was followed by a long pause. Finally, I said, 'I met your brother on the street. I wanted to interview you. I am a reporter at a newspaper.'

'Ah, yes.' His facial expressions remained the same, soft and unruffled. He shifted his gaze to the floor and the awkward pause resumed. When he finally looked up, he let out a deep sigh, 'So what do you wish to ask us?'

'I... I did not really prepare... I just saw him... your brother on the road...' I said.

That face, those shoulders, still undisturbed.

Finally, I said, 'I think I would ask you, most importantly, how you respond to people who say you are an impostor...'

I let the sentence drop. It took me a moment to realize what I had just said.

But to my surprise, the smile on that face broadened. He heaved out another sigh, 'Yes, that is true. There are people like that.'

Silence again. I noticed the Bird of the Death fidgeting in a corner. Will he shoot me now? His brother though was still smiling.

I felt sweat gathering on my brow but I didn't say anything.

He finally said, 'Yes, you are right, my friend. There are people who say such things. But what can you say to such people?'

I couldn't tell if he was asking me or what. I stayed quiet.

'Yes, there are such people, you are right. But there are people who say there is no God, no spirit, no spirituality… And they give you very good reasons to believe them. You can believe those reasons if you want.' Then he added softly, 'But these are all people who do not see. And people who come to us are all suffering from blindness. With the help of God, we cure their inabilities to see and hear.' He stopped and stared at me, 'We all lose our ability to hear when there's too much noise inside. We can't see, can't hear what's outside. Like *you* my friend. You cannot see.'

Then he asked, 'Are you _____ bhai's son?'

It took me a moment to realize that he had just uttered my father's name. I sat there utterly shocked. He knew my father and somehow recognized me too. I had no way to say how.

'How… do you know?'

He smiled. 'We knew him well,' he paused and shifted his gaze to the ground. 'He was a good man. He could see things. You should try to be like him.'

'I am sorry but you will have to excuse us,' he said. 'There are people waiting for us. But you should come at a good time. Give us a call. We'd love to speak with you.

Please don't leave without having some tea. You are our special guest.'

He gestured to his servants who pushed his box toward the curtain. I stood up and watched him leave. As he was about to exit, he turned his head slightly toward me, 'Oh, for next time, please come with a photographer. People like to read interviews with photographs in them.'

The Bird of Death was sitting on one of the charpoys. He came into my view as the wheel-fitted trolley glided across the room towards the other room where I assumed the people were waiting.

'I will show you the way out,' he said. He had taken off his cloak and bag and looked strange and ordinary. We walked out of the house and he asked me, 'So are you really _____ bhai's son?'

'Yes.'

'He was a great man, you know,' he said, pointing me out of the lane. 'He used to come here to perform. I was a kid then.' Then he laughed, his voice eager and childlike. 'You might be taking me for just an advertisement on the road, but I got into this business because of your father. He was not an ordinary performer with magic tricks. He was different. He told us stories. I learned about stories from him and that's what I do myself now. Once you tell somebody a story, you are all in the same world and you can all speak to each other about the same things and understand the same things. _____ bhai used to do strange tricks I have never seen anybody else do. He made sculptures of smoke! Can you imagine, *sculptures*! We had nicknamed him "Jahaz" around here. He imitated sinking ships, sputtering out smoke as they sank.'

I knew what he was talking about. My father died spitting blood because of that smoke.

'But how did your brother know I was his son? I have never come here before.' I said.

He laughed dismissively, 'He's God's man. We all have veils on our sight. He doesn't. In one glance, he can see generations of your family tree, and oh, here's your ID card,' he said, handing back my ID card.

We turned into a narrow lane and suddenly I realized that he was surrounded by a swarm of kids who had been standing around the water hand-pump at the other end of the lane. They all carried buckets and cans and bottles in their hands: pink, yellow, green, blue... When they spotted him, they ran like mad. *Ballee! Ballee!* they yelled, their buckets and cans flying behind them like balloons.

Ballee, become a bear na? Make that sound...

Ballee, swing me in your arms? Please please please...

Ballee, become an airplane, fly for us again, Ballee?

He dropped his bag and lifted the smallest kid in his arms, who immediately complained: *Ballee, what did you become in the bazaar today? Ballee you said you're going to show me what you became. I waited for you...*

Ballee—the Bird of Death—with a child in his arms

looked toward me smiling embarrassedly. He put the kid down, and then told them he would come to play with them in the evening and become a bear, airplane, butterfly, shooting star, and collapsing building. All right, an eagle too. Okay, okay, that as well...

We were startled by a loud honk. A Suzuki mini-van, just a couple of feet less broad than the width of the lane itself, was coming straight at us at an uncomfortably constant speed. The driver had his hand on the horn and did not seem to believe in brakes. The children scampered against the uneven walls of the lane.

~

It was evening. The moon was a lovely pink. As I stood waiting for the bus, I was filled with a sense of wonder. What the man in the box and Ballee said was true: Reasons were invented, and stories were reasons that allowed us to connect ourselves to the world, to compose ourselves in ways that others could read. Fragments were true; but we needed stories greater than fragments. We needed stories in order to imagine the mad world we lived in.

I waved to a bus. My dread and fear had been replaced with an enormous sadness for things that I had lost. I realized that was the difference between my father's stories and mine. He told stories to find ways into the world, to communicate with it. I wrote to avoid the world.

The bus had only a few passengers. I rested my head

against the rusted steel bars of the window and listened to the conductor shouting out the stops the bus was going to make. *Nayee Karachi, Sakhi Hasan, Waterpump, Hyderi...*

Yes, this city was unknown and the noise was great. But this scatter must be gathered.

You are listening.

Acknowledgements

I DO NOT EXAGGERATE: one of the biggest joys of publishing this book is to be able to thank all the various people who have made it possible for me to write. I wish there was a way to show my gratitude to them; here, I offer a mere nod to their generosity and kindness.

My work is, will always be, a tribute to my teachers, who have always been exceedingly patient, generous and kind toward me. Their collective warmth and support over the years has enabled me to muddle through life, literature, and other things I am passionate about. Foremost among them: Kamila Shamsie—my first writing teacher, who, eight years later, was also the final reader of this manuscript before it went out to publishers. There is no way to thank you, K, for your support and friendship. I only hope this book could show just a fraction of all the goodness you have showered upon my work over the years.

Rahat Kazmi, who introduced me to great works of

literature and to this day continues to lend me his books, and for being the example of a broad, ideal reader, who knows all novels in Urdu and English languages (translations included) and is ever-eager to talk about literature, Urdu poetry, William Faulkner, Great books and ideas. Thank you Sir, for continuing to remind me of the vastness of my *jahalat* and the work I have to do to lessen it to whatever degree possible.

Dr. Saeed Ghazi at Lahore University of Management Sciences (LUMS)—my teacher, colleague, friend—whose lectures, classes are some of the best I have attended and who presented to me countless books and articles when I could afford little. Thank you, Saeed. It is impossible to meet the standards of generosity you have set inside the classroom and outside.

At Columbia I was very fortunate to be in the company of extraordinary writers who helped me better myself as a reader and writer, and continually inspired with their remarkable commitment to the enterprise of fiction. Above all: Ben Marcus, Richard Locke, Jaime Manrique, and Zadie Smith. Thank you also to Rob Spillman, who, during the writing of my thesis, helped me unlearn a lot of bad MFA tricks and remain true to the story.

The book went through many stages and at every stage I was blessed to have trusted readers who read the book and pointed out its many flaws. Azeen Khan saw it from its roots to its shoots. Nadeem Aslam, Alisa Ganieva, Taymiya R. Zaman, and Kamila Shamsie read the final iteration of the manuscript and offered insightful feedback and suggestions.

A very special thanks to Mehreen Zahra-Malik for editing my work with loving attention for many years. It has taught me more about prose than I could reckon. I also owe thanks to David Rogers who appeared out of the blue to read the initial versions of the manuscript. He sent it back to me with invaluable feedback, which greatly improved the work.

It has been a pleasure working with enthusiastic editors who believed in the book and helped better it in so many ways: Tim Duggan at HarperCollins, Meru Gokhale and Faiza S. Khan at Random House India, and Dan Franklin at Jonathan Cape.

The unwavering enthusiasm with which Clare Alexander championed the book and stood behind it has been nothing short of amazing. It's been a pleasure and a privilege to have her as representative and advocate. Thank you, Clare.

The Fulbright Scholarship program in Pakistan made it possible for me to undertake an MFA at Columbia University when I had an admission offer but no money; so, thank you to the USEFP for the funding and help. Can Serrat Residency, El Bruc, Spain—allowed me the time and space for 30-days to mull over how to bring together the various pieces of the book and meet some warm, wondrous people. Thank you, Marcel and Karine.

A book emerges in part out of the life one lives: my

abundant gratitude for my friends on whom I depend upon for life-enhancing conversations, ideas and laughter. You are the sustainers of my soul, my dear Azeen Khan (amazing reader, friend, critic), Ali Aftab Saeed (my life-line in Lahore), Ali Sethi (music and friendship), Faiza S. Khan (for Karachi afternoons, long conversations, unceasing laughter over the years), Aurangzeb Haneef (LUMS/PDC/sane advice), Hasan Karrar and Spenta (marvelous neighbors, history and literature conversations, Bahar/Tara), Manan Ahmed (Lahore, Berlin, NYC, walks, space, history, Empire, life, literature, books) and Daniel Wallace (for all hostilities and love over the years).

A book, above all, is a conversation with other books and stories. And storytellers would fail if they did not fulfill their responsibility toward stories that helped them understand the world and themselves better. I owe a lot to Naiyer Masud's writings, who is among the greatest fiction writers in Urdu. I met *Jahaz* in his story Sheesha Ghat. It is an honour to have an incarnation of him in my story *Things and Reasons*. The line quoted on page 1: *'name the streets and number the dead'* is from Harris Khalique's searing poem, *I Was Raised in Karachi*. Musharraf Ali Farooqi's extraordinary translations of *Tilism Hoshruba* and *Dastan-e Amir Hamza* (*The Adventures of Amir Hamza*) reintroduced me to these stories and helped me reconnect with them in a way that is fundamental to my work here. I owe a debt of gratitude to him for these works and for his support for my work over the years.

These stories, with all their warts and faults, are for my friend and comrade:

Umair Ibrahim with whom I have learned so much, including my humour—

یقیں جو غم سے کریم تر ہے

سحر جو شب سے عظیم تر ہے

www.vintage-books.co.uk